The Autobiography

— of —

Meatball
Finkelstein

The Autobiography
— of —
Meatball
Finkelstein

Ross Venokur

Delacorte Press

Published by
Delacorte Press
an imprint of
Random House Children's Books
a division of Random House, Inc.
1540 Broadway
New York, New York 10036

**Visit us on the Web! www.randomhouse.com/kids
Educators and librarians, for a variety of teaching tools,
visit us at www.randomhouse.com/teachers**

Library of Congress Cataloging-in-Publication Data

Venokur, Ross.
 The autobiography of Meatball Finkelstein / by Ross Venokur.
  p. cm.
 Summary: Thirteen-year-old Meatball, an overweight vegetarian,
discovers that eating meatballs gives him the magic power of turning
into anything he wants, and he uses this ability to fight his
principal's diabolical plot to eliminate fun from the planet.
 ISBN 0-385-32798-6
 [1. Magic—Fiction. 2. Overweight persons—Fiction. 3. School
principals—Fiction. 4. Schools—Fiction. 5. Vegetarianism—Fiction.
6. Humorous stories.] I. Title.
PZ7.V562 Au 2001
[Fic]—dc21
                                                              00-056958

The text of this book is set in 12-point Dutch Aster.

Book design by Trish P. Watts

Manufactured in the United States of America

May 2001

10 9 8 7 6 5 4 3 2 1

BVG

*For my dad, who, among so many other things,
took me to the barber and taught me to say
"Meat-a-ball"*

1

Dear Diana Capriotti:

I got the letter. You're right, that's a generous offer. What can I say but yes? Yes, I'll tell you about my secret. I'll tell you the truth about principals and about the principal principal and his principle, the Principal Principal's Principle, as you may have seen it in the papers. I'll tell you about the FV, the PWO, the PPP, and the PTA. Basically, I'll tell you about every single thing that happened to me last week. But first, I'm going to tell you about my name, because everyone's always interested in that. Besides, it's the beginning of my story.

Thirteen years ago from two weeks from last Tuesday, Babs Finkelstein spent most of the morning and all of the afternoon and evening lying on a delivery room table screaming her head off. Her husband, on the other hand, didn't make a sound. Harvey Finkelstein could barely breathe. This was only the second time he had been through childbirth, the third if you count his own. Either way, this wasn't how he remembered it.

Two years earlier, Harvey and Babs's first child, Precious Finkelstein, quietly popped into the world in the middle of the afternoon. Six pounds and nine ounces of perfect baby girl. Precious's arrival was as uneventful and painless as any mother could hope for. Nothing like the trauma Babs was experiencing now.

Helpless, Harvey did what he was best at. He paced back and forth with his two-year-old daughter in his arms. Hours later, after Harvey wore a hole in the sole of his left loafer, Babs pushed out the Finkelsteins' new baby—the biggest, roundest, fattest baby the world had ever seen. A twenty-seven-pound, four-ounce freak of nature. Me.

My mom and dad burst into tears. Of joy? I've never been dumb enough to ask. And though they sobbed, my precious sister, whom I had not even been introduced to yet, giggled, pointed and said her first word ever. Not "Mommy." Not "Daddy." "Meatball." How precious is that?

Precious is perfect. She's a straight-A student, she's fluent in three languages, she's popular, she's president of two million extracurricular activities, she's a poet, she's a French horn player, and she's even something of a chef. She has perfectly straight blond hair with a perfect flip right above her shoulders. And, as my mom is always quick to point out to anyone who'll listen, Precious's perfect curl perfectly complements her perfectly adorable freckles on her perfect button nose, which sits beneath the most perfectly clear blue eyes ever created.

I, on the other hand, look like a meatball. My face is round. My body's round. Basically, *I'm* round. Which, of course, means fat. My mom prefers *big boned*, while my dad wants me to believe that *I'm still growing into myself*. And though they and my sister are all tall, thin, blue-eyed blonds, I ended up with marinara-red hair and seared-beef-brown eyes. It's hard to believe I'm even related to these people. But I am, which gives me the distinguished honor of being the only imperfect thing in Precious's otherwise perfect life—and if there's one thing my sister can't handle, it's imperfection.

Poor Precious could never figure out what to do with me. Part my hair to the left or to the right, put me in a hooded sweatshirt or put me in a sweater vest, give me glasses or give me contacts, and I'm still a fat kid named Meatball. There's just no escaping it. So it was only a matter of time before Precious had to face the simple truth: I would never be perfect. And as far as Precious was concerned, if I couldn't be perfect, I couldn't *be*. Period. So she started to pretend that I didn't exist.

The silent treatment began when I was in kindergarten. It was a Monday morning. My sister kept up her Meatball Acknowledgment Embargo until the maple bookshelf fell off the wall and pinned her leg to the ground. We both knew that Precious had only one choice. Actually, she could

have waited six and a half hours for my parents to get home from work. And to be fair, she tried. But after an hour and a half, the pain became unbearable and she asked me for help. That was on a Wednesday, two and a half years later.

The next morning, the second embargo started, and it hasn't let up once in the last seven years. It's like my mom and dad tell anyone who sets foot in their market, "When our Precious sets her mind to something, she does it perfectly, every time."

Nine years ago, when I was four, my mom and dad decided to fulfill their life's dream. They quit their boring government jobs and opened a tiny health food market called

Tofu For-u
Celebrating You and Tofu.

I don't know exactly when my parents got on their health kick, but it was sometime before Precious and I were born, because neither of us has ever

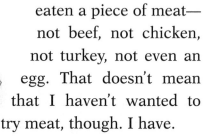

eaten a piece of meat— not beef, not chicken, not turkey, not even an egg. That doesn't mean that I haven't wanted to try meat, though. I have.

In third grade, I woke up one night in the middle of a dream about a corned beef on rye the size of the Empire State Building, with a Chrysler Building–sized side order of chicken parmigiana, and I stumbled into my parents' bedroom.

"Is everything all right?" my mom worried.

"Uh-huh." I nodded. "Why don't we eat meat?"

"Meatball." My mom took my hand in hers. "If we were intended to eat animals"—she smiled softly—"they would be covered in ketchup. Now go back to bed."

Regardless of when and where the vegetarianism began, it seemed to pay off when Mom and Dad opened their dream market's doors to enormous success. The market grew more and more prosperous each year until, in its fifth year, Tofu For-u attracted the attention of

SUPER HEALTH
The Supermarket for Our Nation's Super Health Needs.

Once Super Health's corporate headquarters got wind of my parents' success, they did what they do best. They opened one of their megastores right across the street from Tofu For-u and stole all Mom and Dad's customers.

Nowadays, I almost never see my parents. They're always working, or having some meeting at a bank, or off attending some small business owners' conference in a place like Tallahassee. And when they are home, they're in their bedroom with the door closed and their voices down so that I can't hear what they're saying, which makes it really difficult for me to hear what they're saying. I have to get all my information through the air-conditioning vents. The other day I heard them say something about $37,816.14. I couldn't figure out exactly what they were talking about, I just knew it wasn't good.

I tiptoed past my parents' room to talk to Precious about it. She may love to pretend I don't exist, but when it comes down to it, family is family. I hoped that what I had to say would finally put an end to the seven-year Meatball Acknowledgment Embargo. Instead, she chased me out of her room with a stick without uttering a single word. She's that good.

You don't believe me? Ask Max, he'll tell you.

The moment Max walked into my second-grade class, I learned that there is something worse than being the new kid at school: being the one-armed new kid. Two months before he showed up at Parkman, Max and his mom grabbed a cab uptown to meet his dad. Without looking, the cabbie pulled out into traffic, and the next thing Max knew, he was in a hospital bed, but his right arm wasn't. Fortunately, Max's mom was not hurt. Don't feel bad for him. He hates that.

Besides, I never feel bad for him. At first, it was simply because I was too busy feeling bad for myself to worry about anyone else; but now it's because of the Cabbie Pact. After we met, it only took Max one week to become so completely fed up with my round-the-clock personal pity party that he looked me in the eye and said, "Get over yourself!"

"That's easy for you to say," I whined. "You don't look like me. You're a normal-sized kid, with normal brown hair, with normal green eyes, with a normal name, with—"

"One arm!" Max reminded me.

"What about that?" I had been dying to ask him

this question since we met: "Your arm got ripped off two months ago—why are you always in such a good mood?"

"Because," Max replied, "I'm not the cabbie."

"What does that mean?" I asked.

"The cabbie's dead."

"Oh" was my brilliant response.

And that's when we made the Cabbie Pact. Max and I resolved that from that moment on, we'd never feel bad for ourselves or for each other. We were alive, we had a lot to be happy about, and we weren't going to waste our time sitting around being depressed. Now everything's nice and simple. Max is my best friend, and I'm his right-hand man—not that he needs one.

Before Max lost his arm, he was a righty. So when he showed up in second grade and the rest of us were learning how to write cursive, he had to learn how to print all over again with his left hand. "The only hand I have left," Max joked. It was amazing. He never got frustrated. And by the end of second grade, he wrote cursive just as well as I did. By the end of fifth grade, Max was our Little League team's best pitcher. Last year, he took up painting, and wouldn't you know, he's great at that, too? Come to think of it, he's a lot like Precious. Maybe that's why I like him so much. Don't tell Precious I said that.

The only other person Max and I ever talk to is my gramps, and he can't hear a word we say since he's been deaf forever. He can read our lips, though, and he taught us both sign language. To be honest, I'm still figuring it out, but Max is a pro. If you're ever looking for me, chances are I'll be at Gramps's place. He lives two floors below the rest of us, and I'm down there all the time.

Gramps is the only grandparent I have. My grandma died before I was born. She had one of those awful diseases that parents don't like to say around their children. And my other grandparents were hit by a stray shot put at the '92 Summer Olympics. We saw the whole thing on TV, along with the rest of the world. The government of Romania still sends us flowers and local cheeses every year on the anniversary of their death.

Actually, that's what woke me up last Monday morning. The flower guy was ringing Gramps's buzzer, which Gramps, being deaf, obviously couldn't hear. He has a light hooked up to the doorbell, but he didn't notice it last Monday morning since he was sleeping too. I pulled myself off the couch, told the flower guy he had the wrong Finkelstein ("This is the Finkelstein on twelve. You

want my parents—the Finkelsteins on fourteen."),
and realized that I was already fifteen minutes late
for school. I only mention all of this now because
last Monday was the day everything went nuts.

Parkman is no different from any other school. It
has studs, it has geeks, it has jocks, it has dweebs,
it has babes, it has dorks, it has a world-class,
award-winning bully, Rufus Delaney, and it has
that one kid who Rufus and everyone else loves to
pick on—me. At Parkman, a day at school isn't
complete unless it begins with one of Rufus Delaney's morning sessions.

A session occurs in five or six parts, depending
on how much time we have. Part One, "The
Shock!", is designed to disorient me. For instance,
I'll walk into school in the morning and Rufus will
drop down on me from the ceiling, or I'll open my
locker and Rufus will pop out and whack me in
the gut, or I'll be walking down the hall and an orange will smash into the side of my head. As I re-
cover from the shock, "The Assembly" begins.

Rufus brays like the donkey he is and blurts out something brilliant like "What's the matter, Meathead?" The thing is, it doesn't matter what he says. He just has to say it loud enough to attract our classmates, who then assemble to see what's going on. Normally Rufus throws in a couple of extra-loud brays at this point to give stragglers and late-comers a chance to join the festivities.

Part Three of the session, "Hey, Fatso," gives Rufus the opportunity to try out his latest fat jokes on me. Regardless of the setup, the jokes all have the same punch line: I'm fat. The hilarious subject of my weight beautifully segues into Part Four, "Your parents actually named you Meatball?" Much like Part Three, the jokes of Part Four all have one punch line: My name's Meatball. Somewhere between Part Three and Part Four, I begin to wish I were dead and wonder to myself why nasty kids like Rufus love making fun of fat kids like me. I don't know the answer to that question. I just know that being named Meatball doesn't help.

Part Five, "And you're a vegetarian!", is a perfect capper to "Your parents actually named you Meatball?" Like my weight, there's nothing that funny about being a vegetarian, unless, of course, you're a vegetarian named after a ball of meat.

Most of the time, the bell mercifully rings some-time during Part Five, and Rufus is forced to re-treat to his corner until the bell rings again at three o'clock, when he comes out fighting. How-ever, if we happen to get a particularly early start in the morning, he always tries to make a little time for Part Six, "Pain."

Rufus is a big fan of pushing me over things. So far this year, he's pushed me over a box, a garbage can, a backpack, a kindergartner, a wall, a chair, a desk, a mom, a bike, a car, a bench, a table, a pumpkin, a fire hydrant, a bar, a piñata, a dog, and a hot dog vendor. He also enjoys pulling on my chubby cheeks and prodding me in the stom-ach with his finger like I'm that little doughboy who sells dinner rolls on TV.

Of course, my assembled classmates like to join Rufus by hurling out their own insults during my sessions. I have no idea why they hate me. "The good news is," I once tried to tell Max, "I don't really care."

"You're lying." Max called my bluff.

"I know." I immediately caved, as is my style. "I just don't get it. It's not my fault that I'm fat. I mean, I was more than twenty-seven pounds when I was born."

"I know." Max put his arm around me. "No one

actually hates you because you're fat. Well, maybe Rufus does, but he's barely human, so he doesn't count."

Max was right. Rufus is barely human. So I guess the real question is not why do my classmates hate me so much, but why do they support him? He slobbers when he speaks. He spends all day scratching at his matted brown hair, which he hasn't washed since ever. He smells bad. All he ever does in class is gnaw on his pencils. And he's at least two feet taller than the rest of us. He's like some freaky hybrid of Frankenstein and Shirley—that's Max's basset hound.

Here's the strangest part of it all: Though my classmates rally around Rufus during sessions, they don't like him any more than they like me. The girls talk all the time about how foul he is. Precious even stopped speaking to one of her friends for over a month once because that friend spread a rumor that Precious wanted to marry Rufus. And the guys are just as bad. They're always telling stories about Rufus when he isn't around.

"I heard Rufus's mom ate his dad for dinner, and that she served one of the legs to Rufus."

"That's impossible, because Rufus's dad shoved Rufus's

mom into a cardboard box and mailed her to Australia, and no one has seen her since."

"That's impossible! Rufus's mom is president of the PTA. In fact, she adopted Rufus just so she could get the job."

"You're all wrong! Rufus keeps his mom and dad chained up in his bedroom closet and feeds them dead pigeons he finds in the park."

It's strange—everyone's always talking *about* him, but no one ever talks *to* him. When he speaks, people just smile awkwardly and nod like they're afraid he'll kill them if they upset him. Maybe that's why everyone rallies around Rufus whenever he's in the middle of a session. They want to stay on his good side.

Rufus has experimented with other subjects, but I draw the largest crowds, most likely because, besides Max, I have the fewest number of friends. Actually, now that I mention it, Rufus tried to put Max through a session once, but, man, was that a failure. Half the kids wanted Rufus to leave Max alone because it was baseball season and, like it or not, Max is the best pitcher Parkman has, and the other half thought it was just wrong to pick on the one-armed kid. What I'd like to know is, how come it's not just wrong to pick on the fat kid?

Anyway, when the Romanian flowers and

cheeses arrived last Monday, I was already fifteen minutes late for school, way too late for the morning session. I walked by Rufus on the way to my desk, and I made sure to smile big, which irritated him to his core. I could just tell Monday was going to be a great day. Boy, was I wrong.

Shortly after I took my seat, Principal Walrus W. Weaselman, or "Valrrruz Doubleju Veazelman," as he calls himself, walked into our classroom. Principal Weaselman, or Veazelman, or "the Weaselman" as us kids call him, is a force that no one with a brain would stand up to. He is universally feared and hated. No one likes him. Not kids like me, not kids like Rufus, not kids like Precious, not even the teachers.

He has the cold, hard personality of a bowling ball, and the looks to match. He's completely bald. His lipless mouth is always shut, even when he's screaming at some poor kid who probably didn't do anything wrong. He has dark gray squinty eyes, and when he moves, his dark gray suit, dark gray shirt, and dark gray tie bunch up to match. He even smells like a bowling ball—well, more like bowling shoes, actually. He stinks.

The strangest thing to me about the Weasel-man is that he's the principal of a school. He hates kids. He openly despises us. Why would he want to spend all his time surrounded by us? My own personal theory is that he became a principal because it's the only job in the world that allows an adult like him to legally torture large numbers of children. And believe me, that's a right that he exercises to the fullest.

Before Max and I even entered junior high, we had heard the story of Principal Weaselman and Nicholas Bogaty. Supposedly, a few years ago, the Weasel-man locked this Nicholas kid in a duffel bag with only one tiny airhole because he was wearing plaid pants. That night the kid told his parents what happened. But his parents, who had graduated from Parkman long ago, were too afraid of the principal to confront him, so they just told their son to get a new wardrobe. I don't know if that story is true. Heck, I don't even know if Nicholas Bogaty ever existed. I do know that no one ever wears plaid pants to Parkman.

Another time, not too long ago, when I was listening to my parents through the vents, I heard my dad say, "I don't get it. Precious has perfect grades. She's far and away the best student at Parkman. Why hasn't she ever earned an award, or recognition of some sort?"

"Honey," my mom said to soothe my dad's bruised nerves, "we've been through this before. Principal Weaselman doesn't believe in praising or commending children for anything. And you know what? It's probably for the best."

"How so?" my dad challenged.

"A ceremony in honor of Precious's outstandingness would just put more undue pressure on Meatball." My grades, as you may have guessed, are less than perfect.

"Still," my dad argued, "that's a pretty lousy policy."

"What do you expect?" my mom asked. "He's a lousy man. That's why his wife left him."

Yep, the Weasel-man was actually married once. But my mom had it backward. The way I heard it, the Weasel-man left his wife the day she told him she was thinking about having kids. The story goes that when she came crawling back a week later, claiming that she didn't know what had come over her and that she didn't need children to be happy, good ol' Valrrruz wouldn't take her back. He said he could never be with someone who considered having children, even if it was only for a moment. Then he dropped his wedding ring in the garbage disposal right in front of his wife and made her listen as it was chopped to pieces.

Nowadays, the only ring the Weasel-man wears is around his thumb. It's a wide silver band engraved with the image of a crying child in thick chains. Like I said, why this man became a principal is beyond me.

Understandably, I'd say, the very sight of the Weasel-man frightens the bejeezers out of me. Still, I was hit with a wave of excitement when he peered into my classroom last Monday morning. It had nothing to do with him, though—it had to do with what he brought with him.

"Mz. Nizami," Principal Weaselman squealed at my teacher in his little pig voice, "I apologize, but I am being forced to stick you vith a new student despite my objection that the lazt thing thiz school needz iz anotherrr mizerable kid. Still, she'z yourz now. Do with herrr vhat you vill. That iz all." The principal clicked his heels together, spun around, and marched out of our room, leaving the new girl alone in the doorway.

"The new girl," as everyone called her that day (as in "Have you seen the new girl? She just moved here from someplace like Zimbabwe"), was Jessica George, the girl with two first names, one girl's and one boy's. There's also a kid in our school named Jeffrey David, but he has nothing to do with the story.

Ms. Nizami Pastrami—that's what everyone calls my English teacher since she always has slabs of deli meat hanging off her chin after lunch period—assigned Jessica the only empty seat in our class. I watched Jessica's sandaled feet pitter-patter across the floor, studied her root beer–brown ponytail bopping up and down, and marveled at her glistening grass-green eyes. A terrifically wonderful, dreadfully awful thought popped into my head. "The only empty seat in this entire room is right next to me!"

A bead of sweat formed on my forehead and darted down my face. My left leg came to life and wiggled back and forth uncontrollably. My saliva packed up and left town. Alone, my tongue pruned up. This wasn't fair! No one had warned me that this beauty would show up in my class. No one had notified me that Nizami Pastrami was going to assign her the seat next to mine. Had I known, I would have prepared an interesting monologue, or an impressive pastry, or maybe a diorama of Notable Jessicas Throughout History—something. This wasn't fair!

In my entire career of peer abuse and humiliation, I had never felt nearly as frightened, or nauseated, as I did when Jessica took her seat next to me. I took a deep breath, and Jessica's sweet Hawaiian Punch scent filled my head. I instinctively looked the other way. What would a girl like her think of a boy like me?

"Man," I thought to myself, "I am so fat."

"What?" I contested. "Who said that?"

"You did, Lard-butt," I told myself.

I had no idea what was happening inside me. I didn't know where those thoughts were coming from. I didn't care about being fat. Did I?

"Ohhh," I thought, "I'm going to puke." I fought so hard to hold back the inevitable that I made myself delusional. I actually believed that I heard the exquisite Jessica George say hello to me. I cautiously turned to face her. She was smiling at me.

Let me repeat that in case anyone missed it. *She* was smiling at *me*. I lost myself in the sparkly silver braces that adorned her adorably crooked teeth like the Queen of England's jewels, and I felt something inside me change.

"Hello," she repeated.

Most of the time, hello is just hello. Last Monday morning, though, when Jessica George said hello to me—to me, of all people—hello was a miracle.

She didn't say "Hey, Fatty."

She didn't say "What's up, Doughboy?"

She didn't say "I didn't know the Goodyear blimp went to this school."

All she said was "Hello."

"Hello," I responded, though not in a voice I recognized. What had happened? My voice was about six octaves lower than the one I'd woke up with. I was prepared to turn around, ashamed, and begin the process of wishing I were dead, but the new girl just kept smiling at me.

Naturally, another wave of nausea hit me. I knew right then that I was in love. That's right, love. Go ahead. Laugh. I'll wait.

Three bites into my braised tofu, onion sprout, and soy muenster pita pocket, Max plopped down beside me at our regular lunch table. "Hey, Meatball. Didn't see you at the morning session."

"I overslept," I managed to splutter, my mouth full. "What happened?"

"Whoa," Max said. "The real question is, what happened to your voice?" I was hoping no one would notice the change. But how could anyone miss it? It was like I had gone from being Princess Leia to being Darth Vader in the course of a morning.

"I don't know," I rumbled in my new voice. "Nothing. Forget about it. What happened at today's session?"

"Rufus gave Ronnie a black eye."

Ronnie Rothman's my number one substitute. In case I'm ever unable to attend any of my regularly scheduled sessions, Ronnie fills in for me. Not by choice, of course. It's just that in the World According to Rufus Delaney, the next funniest thing after a fat kid like me is a hairy kid like Ronnie.

Last year, Ronnie showed up in school one day

with a shadow above his lip. Two weeks later, he had a mustache. Three weeks later, he had sideburns coming in. Four weeks after that, while Ronnie was changing into his gym clothes, Rufus noticed a few hairs on Ronnie's back. And that was that.

I once tried telling Ronnie not to worry about kids like Rufus Delaney. "He's just jealous of people who have more than him," I jokingly rationalized. "Take me, for example. Rufus has always envied me for having more fat than him. Don't know why, he just has. So what if he envies you now for having more hair? It's not our problem, Ronnie." I gave him a friendly pat on the shoulder. "It's Rufus's."

Ronnie shoved me up against a locker, grunted, "Who asked you, Blubber?" and punched me in the gut. I fell to the floor, one hundred percent confident that, deep down, he'd appreciated our little talk.

"Isn't Ronnie's eye still black from last week's session?" I questioned Max now.

"That's his other eye." Max pointed across the cafeteria.

Ronnie was just walking in. His two black eyes matched the shadowy growth above his upper lip. When he scanned the lunchroom in search of allies, he caught me staring. I waved. He gestured back at me.

"You don't need to know sign language to know what that means," Max chuckled.

Max thinks it's funny that I'm always going out of my way to be nice to Ronnie. It's not like I don't know he hates me. That's obvious. But I still feel responsible to him. After all, if I never missed a session, Ronnie would never have to endure one.

"What are you doing after school?" Max asked.

"I was just going to go home and try to trick Precious into speaking to me."

"It's too bad she's such a snot," Max said in the dreamy voice he reserves for his Precious fantasies.

I rolled my eyes. Max has this inexplicable thing for my sister. He actually thinks she's the cutest girl in school. Still, in all our years of friendship, he's only tried to speak to Precious once. What a disaster that was. He was so nervous, he got gassy. When he attempted to say hello, he ended up burping in her face.

"What are you doing after school, Max?"

I think he responded to me, but I didn't hear him. Jessica George, the *actual* cutest girl in school, was walking right toward us.

"Hello," she said to me for the second time that day, and what a day it was shaping up to be.

"Hello," I carefully reciprocated, attempting to keep all tofu inside my mouth.

"Um, hey," Max cautiously responded, not used to anyone other than me speaking to him.

"Do you mind if I sit here?" Jessica asked, smiling at us.

Max and I looked at our table. No one had ever sat in any of the eight other chairs that surrounded it. We didn't even know if they worked.

"No?" I sort of asked.

"Great!" Jessica sat down. Her chair didn't collapse, which I took as a good sign. "I'm Jessica," she told Max.

"Max," Max replied, still a bit confused about who this girl was and why she was at our table.

"And I never got your name," she said to me.

"Meatball," I whispered.

"What was that?"

I whispered again, and again she didn't hear me. I didn't mean to whisper. Honestly. It's just that, all of a sudden, after a lifetime of not caring one way or the other, I desperately wanted my name to be something else. But it wasn't.

I was finally forced to say "Meatball" in an audible tone.

"Meatball?" Jessica challenged, like I was playing some sort of joke on her.

"Meatball." I shrugged.

"Really?" she pressed, holding back a laugh in case I was telling the truth.

"Really," I insisted, my eyes to the floor.

"I never met anyone named Meatball before. Meatball." She pondered my name out loud, trying it on for size. "Meatball. Hmm," she finally concluded, "that's a good name."

"You serious?" I was skeptical, to say the least.

"Of course. My dad calls me Cupcake all the time. What's the difference?"

On the surface, I think I maintained my cool. But on the inside, I was going nuts.

"Holy cow!" I celebrated to myself. "What did I ever do to deserve this? I mean, why is this girl even talking to me?"

"Who cares," I yelled at myself. "She's saying something else, pay attention, sit up straight, and try not to look so big."

"You know what I mean?" she asked.

"I'm sorry," I said, cringing, "what did you say?"

"I said"—Jessica smiled—"that Principal Weaselman's a real jerk."

"You don't even know." Max jumped in before I could embarrass myself further. "Last year he hoisted a kid up the flagpole and left him there all day."

"Why?"

"The Weasel-man didn't like his haircut."

Max laughed. Jessica looked horrified. I just sat there like an idiot and smiled. Of all the tables Jessica could have sat at, she'd sat at mine.

"This is way too good to be true," I rejoiced to myself. "Isn't it?"

As if on cue, a Rufus Delaney–shaped shadow spread over our table.

10

"I'm sorry." Rufus drooled all over his own shirt as he spoke. "I hope I'm not interrupting anything." Rufus's sudden arrival shocked me as well as Max and Jessica. Rufus started braying like the donkey that he is, and before I could even attempt to contain the situation, the regular assembly of onlookers was flocking to our table. I had no choice but to buckle down for an unscheduled lunch session with the radiant Jessica George sitting at my side.

Rufus's pointy yellow teeth gleamed under the cafeteria's fluorescent lights. "We missed you this morning, Meatstick." He cackled to give interested stragglers time to join the group.

"So," Rufus said, slobbering, "you're the new girl, huh?" This was an unprecedented move. Rufus never talked to anyone else when he was working me over. Besides, after his idiot masses had assembled, he was supposed to move on to Part Three and start making fat jokes. "You seem pretty normal," he complimented Jessica, who took a moment to consider how to respond to such lame flattery.

She settled on "Thanks, I guess."

"Let me do you a big favor, New Girl, and give you some free advice that can really add to the quality of your life here at Parkman. You don't want to sit with Meatcube and Max. You're cute, and no one who's cute sits at this table."

I fidgeted in my seat, wiping my sweaty palms on my jeans under the table.

Max sat next to me, motionless.

Jessica looked incredibly uncomfortable.

"Listen," Rufus consoled her, "no one here is going to hold this embarrassing mistake against you. You're new. How could you know you were sitting at the freak table?" He looked at me and Max. "How could you *not* know you were sitting at the freak table?" A real showman, Rufus paused so his fans could laugh. Then he graciously pardoned Jessica. "No big deal. We'll just write this whole thing off as a rookie's mistake, what do you say?" Rufus smiled and some crud fell off his front tooth.

Jessica quivered in her seat and studied Rufus's hideous smile. She glanced up at the crowd that was gathered behind it. All her new classmates were pointing and laughing.

"Do yourself a favor," Rufus persisted, scratching at something crawling around in his matted hair. "Come join the rest of us over there." He gestured across the cafeteria. "Where the normal kids sit."

"Yeah," some other kid shouted, "you're new here, there's still time for you!"

"Just walk away!" Ronnie Rothman, of all people, added.

"You're making the biggest mistake of your life!"

"Get out while you can!"

Poor Jessica. She looked like someone was interrogating her under a hot light. She glanced over at me, but I looked away, hoping that if I couldn't see her, she couldn't see me. She turned to Max, who forced himself to smile, for Jessica's sake, and bravely say, "It's all right. You can go."

Jessica's a great person. Really. But she's also just a person. People don't always make their best decisions under pressure. Look, it was a tough situation for the new girl to find herself in. She did what she thought she had to do to survive. She stood up, picked up her lunch tray, and excused her way through the cruel crowd.

Meanwhile, a craggy smile crept across Rufus's ugly mug, and I knew that the worst was yet to come.

11

Rufus bent over, and when he popped back up, he held a cafeteria tray covered in meatballs. He slammed the tray onto my table, and a few of the meatballs jumped up into the air. I glanced across the cafeteria at the large sign that hung above the door on the first Monday of every month: MEATBALL MONDAY.

"Does anyone know what time it is?" Rufus said, luring the crowd in.

"No, Rufus," the chorus of mindless baboons answered. "What time is it?"

The room became completely quiet. My moronic classmates waited with bated breath, though you didn't need to be a genius to put it together:

1 tray of meatballs
1 kid named Meatball
+ 1 jerk, like Rufus Delaney
_____
= 1 predictable outcome

Still, Rufus milked the moment for all it was worth. He nodded a few times. He looked around from face to face. He even licked his chops like the Frankenstein dog he was. Finally he howled, "It's time for Meatball to eat a meatball!" Thunderous applause threatened to rip the room apart.

Max whispered to me, "What should we do?"

I didn't know.

Rufus Delaney wasn't the first person to try to force-feed me a meatball. I had successfully staved off over a dozen such attempts in my life by well-meaning waiters, curious meat-eaters, less insistent bullies than Rufus, and even Max once or twice in the early days of our friendship. And I had also overcome my own passing desires. Just eight or nine weeks earlier I'd been hit with a wave of curiosity while walking down the street with my mom.

"Mom, what does meat taste like?" I wondered aloud.

"Like diseased death," my mom responded without hesitation.

"Well, what would you say if I told you I want to buy a hot dog from the next vendor we pass?"

"I'd say you're trying to give me a heart attack. Now stop talking crazy."

"How come everyone else I know gets to eat meat and I don't?"

"Meatball," my mom scolded me, "if we were intended to eat animals, they would be garnished with a pickle."

When we walked by the next hot dog vendor, I didn't say a thing. I'm too smart to push my mom. Besides, the desire had passed. It always did. How could I eat meat? It would break my parents' hearts.

But when Rufus shoved that tray of meatballs into my gut, I wasn't looking at my parents, I was looking at Jessica George looking at me from across the room. My mom wasn't there to tell me that if we'd been intended to eat animals, they'd be filled with Worcestershire sauce instead of blood. And even if Mom had been around, it wouldn't have been nearly as compelling an argument as the embarrassment I could see in Jessica's eyes. For the first time in my life, I was embarrassed for myself because I could tell that someone else was embarrassed for me.

"What's the matter, Meatball?" Rufus slapped

me in the side of the head to get my attention. "Afraid to eat one?"

I didn't respond. I was too busy staring at Jessica. I had had no idea this girl existed when the day began, and yet now, somehow, what she thought and what she felt were the only things that mattered to me. I no longer had any control over what was going on inside me. I had lost all ability to regulate my own feelings.

"Do they bring back too many painful memories?" Rufus slapped me again.

"What?" I muttered, and my bass of a voice cracked, revisiting a significantly higher octave for a moment. Rufus exploded in more hideous laughter and whacked me upside the head again.

That's when it occurred to me that my head was throbbing, but not from Rufus. I realized that I had stopped breathing, that my jaws were clamped shut, and that my fists were balled up so tight they were pulsing. I must not have looked well, because Max stood up and put his hand on my shoulder. "Let's get out of here," he suggested.

"You're not going anywhere." Rufus shoved Max back into his chair.

Next thing I knew, I was on my feet, pushing Rufus away from Max. It's one thing for Rufus to mess with me. I'm used to that. But that big dumb ox had no business touching my best friend. "Leave him alone," I said threateningly.

"How cute," Rufus mocked us, "the big Meatball is protecting his little baby." He jutted an elbow into my chest, knocked me back into my seat, and shoved the tray of meatballs into my gut again. "Eat one."

I looked around. My classmates were standing around the table cheering like they were on the fifty-yard line during the final seconds of the Super Bowl. Max, normally an undisturbed bystander at my sessions, was being shoved, pushed, prodded, and flicked by a faction of Rufus's idiot henchmen. Rufus was laughing so hard that a waterfall of drool was cascading over his bottom lip. And that strange Jessica creature who had somehow seized control of my insides was right there, watching the whole thing.

For the first time in my entire life I felt like I had to prove that I wasn't just some fat kid who people like Rufus Delaney could push around. I had to show Jessica that I could beat this moron at his own game. I didn't care about what my mom and dad would say. I didn't care about anything that had happened before, because everything was different now. Without warning, everything had unexpectedly changed, and all I needed to do now was shut Rufus Delaney up. So that's what I tried to do.

I stood up, grabbed a meatball, and swallowed the whole thing.

"Ewww," Rufus screeched, "Meatball just ate one of his own babies!"

Reality dropped back down onto me as quickly as it had flittered away. The taste of the meat on my tongue instantly made me sick. The thought of my parents finding out that I had betrayed them— even though I knew that if we'd been intended to eat animals, they would have been placed on a bed of lettuce instead of feet—made me sicker. And the fact that standing up to Rufus had not affected the situation in the least made me sicker still.

Any shred of hope that my daring act had proved to at least a handful of my classmates that Rufus Delaney was no more than a bully and an imbecile was crushed when one of them screamed, "He's a cannibal!" and everyone else started chanting, "Can-ni-bal, can-ni-bal, can-ni-bal, can-ni-bal . . ."

"You are *a cannibal," I told myself. "How could you eat that? What were you thinking?"*

"I wasn't thinking," I defended myself.

"Tell it to your mom!" I screamed at myself. "Tell it to that meatball's mom!"

The air became thick as Rufus's heartless assembly crowded closer and closer around me and Max. Every breath I took felt like someone was shoving a pair of gym socks down my throat. I was hot, and chilly, and sweaty, and shivering, and nauseated. The room began to spin around me, and as it picked up more and more speed, the clamor of everyone shouting, "Can-ni-bal, can-ni-bal, can-ni-bal!" throbbed in my ears. I became dizzy, I lost all my equilibrium, and I felt myself collapsing. As I crashed toward the cafeteria floor, I mumbled to myself, "This must be what it feels like inside a tornado."

I never hit the ground.

The next thing I remember, I was hanging from a branch of the giant oak that stands in the middle of the Parkman yard. Max was caught up in the swings, Jessica was stuck in one of the basketball hoops, Ronnie Rothman was tied in a knot around a monkey bar, Rufus was swinging from the top of the flagpole, and the one hundred percent, unexaggerated, honest truth is, everyone else who had been in the cafeteria seconds before was now tangled, suspended, or dangling somewhere in our schoolyard.

12

"Attention, pleaze." The Weasel-man's irritatingly high voice rang through the school's P.A. system a few minutes before one that afternoon. "Thiz iz yourrr prinzipal!" The entire school gasped. The last time the Weasel-man had used the P.A. system had been to announce that he would be drawing five random names out of a hat to select five students to expel. The Parkman Five, as our lost classmates have been memorialized, were given ten minutes to vacate the building.

"All studentz," the Weasel-man continued on that Monday afternoon, "are dizmizzed forrr the day on account of the tornado that deztroyed the cafeteria. That iz all."

Normally, I'd be thrilled to get out of school early. Normally, Max and I would wander over to Tofu For-u to say hi to my folks and get some free food. But last Monday just wasn't normal, and the last thing I wanted to do was see my parents, especially my mom.

If a Mack truck fell on my dad's head, there's a good chance he wouldn't notice it. My mom, on the other hand, would somehow sense that the truck was coming hours in advance. She's aware of everything. She's like some sort of ninja hawk. If I went by the market, I'd kiss her hello and she'd smell meat on my breath, or I'd smile and she'd see a piece of meatball wedged between two teeth in the back of my mouth, or she'd detect a microscopic speck of meat lodged under one of my fingernails, or she'd just sense that I was different somehow and wouldn't stop asking me questions until I confessed.

"You're such an idiot!" I chided myself. "How could you do this?"

"I don't know." I practically started to cry.

"Well, you know what you have to do now," I asked myself. "Don't you?"

I did. I had to get home before my parents, pack a bag, and leave town. There was no other choice. If they found out, they'd kill me. If they didn't find out, I'd die from guilt.

"Yes," I told myself, "That's what I'll do. I'll run away."

"But you won't." I called my own bluff.

"I know," I admitted.

I wasn't going anywhere. I'm not cut out for life on my own, braving the streets, roughing the elements. I like warm food. I like my bed. I like the lock on our front door. I like knowing that my sister is in the next room, even if she won't talk to me. And I like listening to my parents through the vents. Why did any of that have to change? My parents didn't need to find out about the meat. I'd make sure of it.

It's not as though everyone in the city was talking about how a fat kid ate a meatball that day. That's hardly newsworthy. Everyone was obsessing over the real story, the tornado. Even Max, which is why I didn't want to see him after school either. It wasn't his fault, it was just that the whole subject of the tornado bothered me. I didn't understand why everyone else had a version of what happened and I didn't. One kid was positive "This happened," but another was sure "That happened." Some of my classmates insisted, "No, no, no, it happened this way," while others argued, "Uh-uh-uh, that way." Then there was me. I had nothing to say. I had no opinion. I couldn't remember the tornado. If I hadn't been so dizzy, I would have doubted whether I'd been there at all.

I went home to lie down and collect myself so that I could attempt to sort through everything from Jessica George to the meatball to being swept up in a tornado. What a day. No wonder I felt like I was going to collapse.

I crashed through my apartment door and headed straight for the sofa. But the sofa wasn't there. Neither was the coffee table, the two chairs that matched the sofa, the stereo, the TV, or the entertainment center that had once housed the now missing equipment. The entire living room was gone. All that remained was a blueprint, drawn out in dust on the floor, of what had once been there. We'd been robbed!

I quickly looked around. Nothing else seemed to be missing. I checked my room. My six dollars was still safely buried underneath my underwear. I surveyed the other rooms. All the thieves had stolen was the living room. I bolted downstairs to Gramps's place.

As always, Gramps was playing solitaire at the kitchen table. He claims that cards are the secret to long life. He and my grandma played canasta together every day for forty years, and when she died, he switched to solitaire. Maybe he's right about cards. He *is* ninety-seven. Then again, his canasta-playing wife died thirty-six years ago.

Without looking up from his game, Gramps signed, "Meatball? What are you doing home so early?"

"Gramps," I screamed. "We were robbed!"

"What?"

"It's true. The whole living room's gone."

Gramps laughed.

"What's so funny?" I was frantic.

"You weren't robbed. Your parents just decided to get rid of a few things."

"Why would they do that?"

"Don't know. Your mom asked if I'd let some movers in at eleven, so that's what I did. Now it's your turn to answer me. What are you doing home? It's one-fifteen."

"The Weasel-man sent us home early because a tornado hit the cafeteria."

"What?" Gramps looked at me like I was kidding. "A tornado hit midtown?"

"No," I explained, "just the cafeteria."

"Are you okay?"

"I'm fine," I assured Gramps, but another wave of dizziness rolled over me and I collapsed into a chair.

"You don't look like you're okay."

"I am." I grabbed my head in my hands to try to stop it from spinning. "I'm just dizzy. I've been dizzy all afternoon."

"From the tornado?" Gramps asked.

"I don't know. I can't remember it. I remember being in the cafeteria right before the tornado. I remember being stuck in a tree after the tornado. I just don't remember the tornado. Weird, huh?"

Gramps shrugged. "Maybe you hit your head."

"It doesn't hurt. It's just spinning. Do you want to hear something bizarre?"

"Always." Gramps smiled.

"Right before the tornado hit, I thought to myself, 'This must be what it feels like inside a tornado.'"

Gramps furrowed his brow. He didn't know what to make of that.

Neither did I.

"I thought it." I was straining to remember something. "Then it happened." Another wave of dizziness bowled into me and knocked the thing I couldn't remember right out of my mouth.

"Gramps," I heard myself say before I could censor myself, "I *was* the tornado."

"I must have misread your lips," Gramps signed. "Did you say you were the tornado?"

"It's like a dream I can't quite put back together. I have the faintest memory of picking up Rufus Delaney and putting him on the flagpole, and enjoying myself."

"Meatball." Gramps was at a total loss. "You're going crazy, aren't you?"

"No. I was moving at least five hundred miles per hour. Yeah, it's all coming back to me now. I went after them all, because I wanted to make them shut up for once! Whoa. I sound nuts, don't I?"

Gramps nodded.

"You have to believe me, Gramps."

"You sure you're not crazy?"

"I *was* the tornado."

"All right." Gramps decided to humor me. "Say, hypothetically, you were the tornado. How did you turn into a weather system and back? And why haven't you done it before?"

They were both good questions.

"Well," I asked, "what else was different today?" Two answers popped out. "Jessica George and the meatball."

"Meatball?" Gramps asked. "What meatball?"

Whoops. Had I said "meatball"? No. That couldn't have been me who'd said "meatball." I couldn't be stupid enough to just blurt out "meatball" to Gramps. Could I?

"What meatball?" Gramps asked again.

I squeamishly squirmed in my seat. No one in the history of the world had ever looked more guilty. There was no turning back now. I took a deep breath, resolved that, like it or not, it was time to come clean, and sloppily signed, "The meatball I ate."

13

Gramps's lower jaw nearly detached from his head. "You ate a meatball?"

I couldn't lie to him. I might not have been able to look at him, but I certainly couldn't lie to him. While I bowed my head, my hands signed yes, and I told him about everything else that had happened between showing up late at school and being force-fed a meatball right in front of Jessica George—all without ever taking my eyes off the floor.

When my mom and dad became vegetarians, they convinced Gramps to do the same. And though I suspected he wouldn't rat me out, I felt awful. I'd betrayed the whole family. Animals are wrapped in fur, not tortillas, but I'd eaten one anyway.

Gramps's slippered feet slid across the kitchen into the pantry. He stomped on the ground, and I looked up at him. He beckoned me over.

The shelves lining the tiny pantry were covered with cans of vegetables, fruits, tofu products, and soy cheeses. Gramps is a master of the art of punishment without words. Maybe it's because he's deaf, who knows? Anyway, rather than lecture me about what vegetarianism means to my mom and dad and the rest of the family, he forced me to study the foods that sustain my family's life, and as I did, something dawned on me.

"I have to tell them."

"Tell who what?" I asked myself.

"Tell Mom and Dad that I ate meat."

"Oh no you don't!" I argued.

"Oh yes I do!" I insisted.

"No!"

"Yes!"

"No!"

"Yes!"

"Don't be a moron," I belittled myself. "What good will telling them do? They're going to hate you!"

"Still, I don't think I can handle the guilt."

"There are other ways to deal with guilt. Give your six bucks of savings to a charity, or spend time with old people, or adopt a blind chipmunk. Just don't tell Mom and Dad!"

Gramps handed me a box of dairy-free Swiss cheese from one of the shelves. It's no secret that I think dairy-free Swiss is the most vile substance in the world. But I'd eaten meat, and now I

had to ritually purify my palate. I tore open the box and unwrapped a limp slice of the fake cheese, and as I raised it to my mouth, I thought, "You know what? This is punishment enough. Mom and Dad don't need to know anything." Before the damp slab of phony cheese crossed my lips, Gramps yanked it, along with the whole package, away from me.

"What are you doing?" he asked, laughing at me. "You hate this stuff."

"I thought you wanted me to wash my mouth out with it."

Gramps rolled his eyes at me. "Is that really what you think of me? Look." He pointed at the pantry wall, at a small black button that was hidden behind the box of dairy-free Swiss. "Go ahead," he urged, "push it."

I pressed the button. The entire wall, shelves and all, dropped into the floor, revealing a massive silver door. "Could this day get any weirder?" I wondered. Clearly, there was only one way to answer that question. I tugged on the enormous handle, and as the door creaked open, a rush of cold air blew past me.

I could not believe what I was looking at. My grandpa had a secret icebox hidden behind his pantry wall, and the thing was stashed full of meat.

14

Name your favorite meat product, and Gramps had some in the freezer behind his pantry wall. He had steaks, burgers, chicken breasts, ground turkey, pastramis, briskets, lamb chops, bolognas, hot dogs, salamis. I was completely beside myself, and next to both of me was my giggling gramps.

"Your mother's a tough lady to say no to," he signed. "I know. I raised her that way. When she told me she'd decided I had to give up meat, I knew better than to argue. I thanked her for pushing her lifestyle on me and paid a few guys from down the street to install this freezer."

Standing in the cold light of Gramps's meat vault, I didn't feel quite so guilty about my earlier encounter with a single meatball. How could I? I was looking at fifty pounds of dead flesh that belonged to my grandfather. If my mom had ever found out about this, Gramps would have never made it to age ninety-seven, no matter how many games of solitaire he'd played.

"Did you ever stop eating meat?" I asked.

"No." Gramps chuckled as he signed. "Why should I? Because your mom and dad tricked each other into becoming vegetarians?"

"What does that mean?"

"Your mom and dad met in college. They took a poetry class together. You know that, right?"

"Yeah." I nodded.

"Well, here's something you don't know: Your dad was too intimidated to ask your mom out. He thought she was too cool for him. So he started wearing lots of black, and he wrote sickening love poetry, and he grew a small beard, and he even wore a beret once."

"No!" I refused to believe it.

"I'm sorry, Meat, but it's true. And when he finally thought he seemed intellectual and sensitive enough for your mom, he asked her out. But a last-minute wave of insecurity hit him, so he slipped in that he was a vegetarian, even though the cheeseburger he'd devoured before class was still sitting in his stomach.

"Face to face with the black-clad hipster your dad was pretending to be, your mom now felt inadequate. So she one-upped your dad and claimed to be a vegan."

"Was she?"

"Hardly. She was living on a diet of scrambled eggs, roast beef sandwiches, and chicken cutlets at the time."

"When did they tell each other the truth?"

"Two and a half years later." Gramps shook his head. "On the eve of their wedding. Your dad confessed everything. Relieved, your mom 'fessed up to her lies. They went out to split a celebratory cheeseburger, but after two and a half years, they couldn't get themselves to eat it."

"That's why I've never eaten meat before? Because my dad wasn't cool enough to get a date? Wow, are all grown-ups that stupid?"

"Most of us," Gramps said, laughing, and he grabbed a package of ground beef and shut the freezer door. I followed him back into the kitchen.

"What's the beef for?" I asked.

"Well," Gramps said, "are we going to test this meatball theory of yours or not?"

"I guess."

"You guess? How else will we ever know if eating a meatball turned you into a tornado?"

I shrugged.

"Call your mom. Make sure she isn't planning on coming down here anytime soon."

Gramps unwrapped the beef, and I called upstairs, without a worry on my mind. It was the middle of the afternoon. There was no way my mom was home. I'd just leave a message.

"Hello?" Precious answered the phone.

"Ha!" I screamed triumphantly. "You spoke to me! You said—"

Click.

"Hello? Hello?"

I called back. This time I knew I'd get the machine.

"Hello?" my mom practically screamed into the phone.

"M-Mom?" I stammered, caught off guard.

"Oh, dear Lord." My mom was practically sobbing. "Where are you?"

"I'm down at Gramps's."

"Gramps's!" I heard my mom clap her hands. "Of course!"

"What are you doing home, Mom?"

"What am I doing home? I heard that a tornado hit my children's school today, what do you think I'm doing home? I'm looking for you. You could have called me or . . ." She abruptly stopped speaking in the middle of her sentence. It was quiet, and I swear I heard my mom sniffing on the other end of the telephone line. She began to speak again, only she wasn't distressed anymore, she was suspicious. "Meatball?"

"Yes." My voice cracked.

"Is something wrong?"

"Wrong?" I gulped. "Um, no, nothing, why, no, nothing's wrong. Oh"—I tried to cover—"you mean the tornado thing. I'm fine, really. I'm sorry if I made you worry."

"Meatball," my mom snapped, "you sound different. What's with your voice?"

"I don't know. When I woke up it sounded normal, but when I opened my mouth this morning, it was different."

"That's not what I meant," my mom snapped. "You sound different, like something's wrong."

"What are you talking about?" I giggled nervously, "I'm not different. I'm the same Meat I was when I left this morning at eight—Meat, yep, that's me, your little Meatball."

"Who ate meat?" my mom gasped.

"What are you talking about?" I panicked. "Who said 'ate meat'?"

"You said 'ate meat,' " my mom huffed.

"No, no, I said this morning at eight, as in eight o'clock."

"Are you sure that's what you said?"

"Yes." I laughed as if this were all just one big wacky misunderstanding.

"When are you coming back upstairs?" my mom suddenly needed to know.

"Hard to say. Gramps is helping me with some homework, and then . . ."

"What?" I yelled at myself. "What then? Oh, I know!"

"I told him I'd go to the grocery store with him . . ."

"Why?" I asked myself before my mom could. "Why would you do that?"

"To help carry his bags," I explained to my mom. "Yeah. So I'll be home when I get there."

"Hold on." My mom sensed I was rushing her off the phone. "I have to answer the other line. Don't hang up. We're not done talking."

My mom clicked over to the other line, and I racked my brain for an idea on how to get off the phone. The more I spoke to my mom, the more guilty I sounded. Two or three more sentences out of my mouth was all the rope my mom was going to need to hang me.

"Meatball." My mom came back on the phone.

"Yeah." I gulped hard.

"That's your father." She sounded somber. "I have to go. There's a problem at the store. I'll see you at dinner."

"Okay." I sighed. "I love you," but she had already clicked back over to the other line.

Gramps double-locked the front door, wedged a towel into the crack between the bottom of the door and the floor to prevent any meaty aromas from escaping, barricaded the door with a chair and a chest, and set the table for me.

I looked at the pile of meatballs. The thought of their awful taste made me retch. "You know what," I said to Gramps, "this is ridiculous." I pushed the plate away from me. "A meatball didn't turn me into a tornado. That's absurd."

"If you say so." Gramps shrugged, picked up a meatball, and took a big bite out of it. "Mmmmm." He licked his lips.

"Besides," I insisted, "the only thing eating a meatball is going to make me is sick."

"I know," Gramps signed, "you're right." He took another bite out of the meatball.

"I mean"—I eyed the plate of meatballs—"Mom and Dad may have become vegetarians for stupid reasons, but they're right. If I was supposed to eat animals, they would be roaming around in barbecues, not in jungles."

"Amen," Gramps agreed, and he tossed the last piece of his meatball into the air and caught it in his mouth. "I guess I better get rid of the evidence," he signed, and he picked up the plate with the other meatballs, walked over to the sink, and held it out over the garbage disposal.

"Wait," I signed.

"Why?" Gramps asked.

I didn't want to eat any more meat. But how could I not test my theory? I mean, I actually believed that I'd been a tornado earlier that day. I needed to know if I was right or if I was crazy.

I walked over and grabbed the smallest meatball off the plate. Though my classmates were not there to taunt me, I actually felt a bit cannibalistic—like a girl named Jennifer would feel before eating a jenny-ball, or a kid named Billy would feel before chomping into a billy-on-a-stick.

"Well?" Gramps asked.

"Well," I rationalized, "I'd be doing a disservice to science not to test the theory. Wouldn't I?"

"Of course you would." Gramps nodded, looking severe. "In fact, I insist, in the name of science, that you eat that meatball."

The meatball went down, but not without a fight. I began to gag the moment it passed my lips. Once it had cleared the back of my mouth, my throat slammed into reverse. It fought the meatball every millimeter of the way, but the meatball could not be stopped, and soon all that remained was the horrible aftertaste of diseased death in my mouth. And the worst part of it all was, nothing had happened. I was still Meatball.

I looked at Gramps.

"You have to think of what you want to become," he signed, reminding me of my own ludicrous theory. "Try and keep it small. No more tornadoes."

I took a deep breath, cleared my head, and tried to conjure up a small image. But I was staring at the poster above Gramps's kitchen table of a man eating a chocolate bar while riding an elephant. Suddenly I didn't feel quite like myself.

I turned to Gramps. His eyes nearly popped out of his head.

"What?" I tried to ask, but all that came out was an ear-shatteringly loud trumpeting sound. I quickly turned toward the foyer to see myself in the mirror on its wall. My butt smashed into the refrigerator (which was easily four or five feet behind me) and knocked it over. My foot hit the ground, leaving a pothole in the kitchen floor and forcing me to stumble forward and knock down the wall separating the kitchen and the foyer. I looked down at a piece of the broken mirror atop a pile of rubble that used to be the wall and found an elephant looking back.

Though I never would have taken Gramps for a

whooper, that's what he was doing. He was whooping with excitement and dancing around me. It was unbelievable. I was right. The fact that I was now an elephant was all the proof we needed. I *was* the tornado that hit the cafeteria.

After such a bizarre revelation, I did what anyone who had just turned himself into an elephant would have done. I teetered back and forth, passed out, pulverized the kitchen table, and nearly crushed my dancing grandfather.

16

When I came to, I was me again. The kitchen, however, no longer resembled the kitchen. The elephant had destroyed it. I tried apologizing, but Gramps didn't care. He just wanted to see me turn into something else.

He handed me another meatball. "Keep it small."

I smiled as the meatball rolled around in my hand.

"What are you smiling about?" Gramps asked.

"Nothing," I lied. I kept thinking about how Jes-

sica George's root beer–brown ponytail bopped up and down when she walked as I chomped down the meatball and thought "skinny." The next thing Gramps and I knew, I was a hundred pounds lighter.

Over the next hour, I turned myself into a chair, a tree, an artichoke pizza, a leprechaun, a dog-sized cockroach, a cockroach-sized dog, Santa Claus, a giant sneaker, the Mona Lisa, a grizzly bear, a motorcycle, Principal Valrrruz Doubleju Veazelman, an ice cream soda, and my mom. Gramps figured out that it took me exactly two minutes and thirty-nine seconds to become me again, which is why we both completely freaked when, as I was forty-two seconds into being my mom, my actual mom rang Gramps's doorbell. She needed to borrow some Vegenaise to finish making dinner.

"Stall her!" Gramps panicked and ran back into the kitchen to conceal our meaty mess.

"Meatball," my mom impatiently hollered, "open up!"

I *was* my mom. How was I supposed to stall her? If I said anything, I wouldn't sound like me, I would sound like her. There was no way out of this one. With a minute and a half to go before the meatball wore off, I heard my mom's key open the bottom lock. I flew into the kitchen.

"Gramps, we're dead!" I said in my mom's voice. "She has her keys!"

Gramps grabbed the meatballs and dumped them, plate and all, into the first thing he could get his hands on, my backpack. He zipped it up and dropped it by the remains of the kitchen table.

The door swung open and there I was, staring at my mom, who was shocked to be staring back at herself. She rubbed her eyes, and I took the opportunity to dive through the side door of the kitchen into the living room. When my mom looked into the kitchen again, she wasn't there. Her father waved.

"I was right," my mom muttered to herself, "this stress is actually driving me crazy." The destruction in Gramps's place registered with her for the first time. "What in the name of all tarnation happened to your apartment, Dad?"

I looked at my watch. If Gramps couldn't keep her away from me for fifty-one more seconds, we'd have to tell her about the meat. Gramps had not lived ninety-seven years to be killed by his own daughter.

"The water main broke," Gramps signed.

"A burst water pipe?" my mom challenged. "A burst water pipe did all this damage? Where's all the water?"

That was a good question.

"Meatball mopped it up for me." Though Gramps didn't miss a beat, it was a horrible answer. My mom would never buy it. She can't even get me to put my dirty underwear in the hamper. I'm a total slob.

"Meatball mopped it all up?" My mom snorted. "My Meatball? I can't even get him to put his dirty underwear in the hamper. He's a total slob. Where is he, anyway?" my mom demanded.

I looked down. I was still my mom. I started to crawl through the living room toward the bedroom.

Gramps must have signed something to Mom, because she said, "What'd he go down the hall for?" Before Gramps could answer, my mom barked, "Dad, with everything Harvey and I are going through right now, this is the last thing I have time for. What's going on here?"

"Nothing," I said as I walked back into the kitchen.

My mom scowled at me.

"Hi, Mom." I was doing a remarkably lame job of playing cool. "When did you get here?"

"Just now." She looked me over like she does when I'm pretending to be sick. "What's going on here, Meatball?"

"You should have seen it. There was water everywhere."

"I thought you went down the hall."

"I did. But I'm back now."

"Why'd you go down the hall?

"Exercise?" I guessed.

"Was that a question or an answer?" my mom demanded.

"An answer?" I asked.

My mom walked through the ruins of the kitchen toward me. "I want you to come upstairs now. You can help me with dinner."

Too suspicious to take her eyes off me, she reached into the pantry and grabbed a jar of Vegenaise off its shelf without looking. If she had only trusted me, she would have seen the enormous silver icebox filled with meat that in all the excitement Gramps had forgotten to conceal. For the first time ever, my mom's innate ability to sense when I've done something wrong actually saved me from a mountain of trouble.

"Come on," she said. "Get your bag."

"I'll just get it later." I shrugged.

"Why? You're standing right next to it."

Behind her, Gramps feverishly urged me to take it.

My mom shot him a fierce look. He smiled back at her like having a water pipe burst open and destroy his apartment was the greatest thing that had ever happened to him.

She turned around in a huff and stormed upstairs. I nervously followed, a backpack full of meatballs slung over my shoulder.

The moment I set foot in our apartment, my mom stared me straight in the eyes. "Meatball, I think it's time for you to tell me what's going on."

I bumbled to get a word, any word, to come out of my big, dumb mouth. Mercifully, my dad blew into the apartment. He looked right over my head at my mom. "We need to talk."

"What's wrong now, Harvey?" Mom asked.

My dad glanced over at me in what I can only guess he perceived to be a subtle way and whispered, "Adult problems," as if my kid ears couldn't hear any words spoken at such a low decibel.

"Oh." My mom forced a smile so that maybe I'd think adult problems meant something good and wouldn't get worried. By the time she'd finished saying "Why don't you go do your homework?" she and my dad were already in their bedroom.

I guess my mom and dad don't think I know that *adult problems* are bad. Sometimes they forget that I'm a kid, not an idiot. Besides, what my kid brain couldn't figure out on its own, my air-conditioning vent was always happy to fill me in on.

"The bank isn't going for it," my dad said. "I practically begged, but they said no hair extensions." In hindsight, maybe he said "no *more* extensions," but it was hard to hear everything through the vents.

"What should we do?" Mom asked urgently. "Where are we going to get $37,816.14 in the next three weeks?"

"We can start with the kitchen."

"You mean sell it to that guy who took the living room set? Do you know that I happened to wander by his store this afternoon and that he's selling our stuff for three times what he paid us?"

"Do you want to hear what I saw today?"

"Do I?" Mom asked.

"I saw Mr. Edwards walking out of Super Health with a week's supply of groceries."

My mom groaned like someone had kicked her in the stomach. Mr. Edwards was supposedly Mom and Dad's most loyal customer.

"What do you say?" Dad asked. "Should we see what we can get for the kitchen?"

"I don't know. Whatever we do, we have to talk to the kids." Then she said, "It's cold in here. Are you cold?"

The last sound I heard was the vent in my parents' room closing, which was fine by me. I had heard enough somber parent talk. Though it may have been selfish, I didn't want to think about their adult problems when I could be enjoying my incredibly unbelievable secret. I actually had a magic power! I could turn myself into anything in the world! What other kid could make that claim? Sure, I had heard stories of some kid uptown with magic freckles, and of some other kid in the suburbs who'd found a sack of magic fortune cookies, but there was no evidence that those stories were true. Not me, though. I was the genuine article. I had a certified, road-tested magic power. I had to tell someone.

Precious was a tempting choice, largely because she was in the room next door, but she'd never listen to me. She'd be too busy throwing things at my head. And if by some miracle she did listen to me, there was the unavoidable detail of the meatballs I had been eating all afternoon.

Obviously, Mom and Dad were off the list too. Even without their adult problems, they'd kill me if they found out I'd eaten meat, no matter what magical effect it had on me. Gramps already knew, which only left Max. But I was afraid to call him just in case someone "accidentally" picked up the phone and listened to our entire conversation. I'm not being paranoid—my mom does it all the time. She thinks I don't know, but I do. Besides, it was six-thirty. Max was at his drum lesson.

There was one other person I could call. I even went so far as to get her number from information. "But what would Jessica say if I picked up the phone and called her?" I wondered. It was a ridiculous question. I mean, what would I say to her? "Hi, Jessica, it's me, Meatball. You know, the fat kid you walked away from at lunch today. No? Not ringing a bell? Come on, I'm that kid who no one likes except for the one-armed guy. Yeah, now you remember. Meatball, the one who you watched get humiliated today. Anyway, I just wanted to tell you that I was the tornado that tore through the cafeteria this afternoon. And how are you?"

There was nothing I could do, no one I could tell. I was going to have to wait until the next day.

18

By the time Max showed up at our lockers the next morning, I was ready to explode. I skipped the hellos and went straight to "I have to tell you the biggest secret ever. Swear you won't tell anyone."

Max looked at me like I was a moron. "Who, exactly, am I going to tell your secret to? You?"

"Good point," I conceded, remembering that we were friendless misfits. "So, here it is . . ." But before I could unload it, an extremely uncomfortable-looking Jessica George walked up.

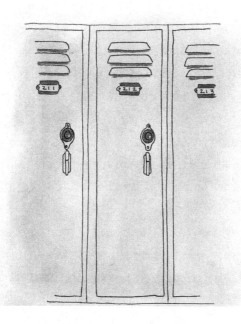

"Hey, guys." Jessica smiled awkwardly. "Can I talk to you two for a second?"

"Sure," we both answered. "What's up?"

"I feel really bad about walking away from you yesterday," she explained. "It's just I'm new, I was overwhelmed . . . You know what, there's no excuse. That's not my line, that's my dad's. We were talking about this last night, and—"

"Extra! Extra!" my brain exploded. "Jessica George was talking about me, Meatball Finkelstein, last night! Extra! Extra!"

"Anyway, I just want you to know that if I could do it all over again, I'd act differently. I'm really sorry."

I wanted to say, "No problem, apology accepted, welcome back, let's hang out, maybe we can go on a date, maybe we can get married, who knows?" But I didn't know how Max felt, so I decided to let him speak first. He must have been waiting for me to speak first, because neither of us said anything, which made Jessica look even more uneasy.

"Well," she said, shrugging awkwardly, "I am sorry. It was a weak moment." She turned around and walked away.

"Hey." Max called her back. "We're the masters of weak moments." I shouldn't have doubted Max. Of course he'd forgive Jessica. And me, I would have forgiven her if she'd stolen her mom's car, tracked me down across ten states, and run me over fifty times.

Jessica smiled and walked back to us. When I saw my reflection in her braces, a calmness settled over me. There was nothing to worry about anymore. She knew my name. She knew what Max and I looked like. She knew what everyone at school thought of us. And still, she was standing in the hallway, smiling at me.

"Meatball." Max nudged me. "Weren't you going to say something?"

"What?" I think I asked Max, though my eyes remained on Jessica.

"The thing." Max was trying to be cryptic.

"Right." I shook off the trance. "My secret."

"Oh." Jessica didn't want to intrude. "I can catch up with you guys later if you want."

"No," I said, "you can hear it too. You just have to promise that you won't tell anybody, ever."

"I promise."

"Okay." The halls were filling with morning traffic, so Jessica, Max, and I huddled up. "Remember the tornado yesterday?"

"Uh-huh." They both nodded.

"It was me." It felt so good to spill the beans. "I was the tornado."

"What are you talking about?" Max was utterly confused.

"When I eat a meatball, I can become anything in the world," I whispered.

Jessica and Max both looked at me like I was a mental case. I recognized the look. It was the same one Gramps had given me the night before. What did I expect? I did sound insane.

"Look, guys," I pleaded, "trust me for now. I'll prove it to you after school."

"No," a horribly familiar voice interrupted. "Prove it to us now!"

I was such an idiot! I was so excited about telling Max my secret that Rufus Delaney's Tuesday-morning session had completely slipped my mind. He did it again. "The Shock" was already over. Only this time, he'd stayed hidden inside my locker long enough to overhear the biggest secret of my entire life.

19

Rufus exploded in a chorus of donkeylike brays, punctuating the end of Part One and the beginning of "The Assembly." My classmates eagerly gathered around to see what Rufus had planned for me that morning. "Did you hear?" he bellowed. "Meatman thinks he has magic powers! Your brain must be as fat as the rest of you, Meatknob!" Another chorus of repulsive laughter attracted all the latecomers before Rufus really sank his teeth into me.

He rattled off yet another impressive succession of fat jokes, but I didn't hear any of them. My ears had stopped picking up outside sounds. They were too focused on the thoughts pulsing through my head.

"Rufus got the best of you yesterday."

"Jessica's going to walk away again if you don't do something."

"Your parents are going to hate you when they find out about this."

"Look at her, she's embarrassed for you. She was embarrassed for you yesterday, too. She's always embarrassed for you."

"I'm embarrassed for you, you fat slob."

"Maybe your parents already hate you. Maybe you are their adult problem."

Annoyed that I wasn't paying attention to him, Rufus shoved me up against a locker. In case that didn't get my attention, he put a hand around my throat and sputtered, "I said, if you really have magic powers, why don't you show us?" A lifetime of not brushing his teeth was beginning to catch up with Rufus. His breath reeked like a rotting roadside squirrel carcass.

Jessica knocked Rufus's hand away from my throat.

He turned to her, howled, "Big mistake, New Girl," and pushed her to the ground, which thoroughly irritated me. The way I saw it, there was only one thing I could do. I reached into my backpack, grabbed one of the meatballs Gramps had hidden in there the night before, and popped it into my mouth, right in the middle of the hallway, in front of everyone.

Here's an interesting little fact about Rufus Delaney that Max once told me. Max's mom and Rufus's mom work together in a bank uptown, and Max's mom once offered Rufus's mom two tickets to the circus because Max had the chicken pox and couldn't go. Rufus's mom politely declined, explaining that Rufus suffered from coulrophobia. Max and I had to look that up. Coulrophobia is an irrational, life-threatening fear of clowns.

I had known this fun fact for a little over a year, but I had never used it against Rufus once. To be honest, I wasn't taking the moral high ground, I was just waiting for the perfect time. Could there ever be a more perfect time?

The next thing Rufus Delaney, and everyone else in the hallway, knew, I was gone. The biggest, meanest, ugliest, nastiest, creepiest clown any of my class-mates had ever seen stood in my place. I had razor-sharp teeth sticking out of a jagged green-and-yellow smile, my hair and nails were bloodred, I was ten feet tall, and all I wanted to do was give a hug to one very special little boy named Rufus.

Rufus screeched like a little girl who'd just found a mouse in her shoe, turned around, and ran straight out the front door of the school so quickly that the track coach spent the rest of the day trying to find him to sign him up for the sprinting team. By the time I turned back into Meatball, everyone else, aside from Max, had run off too. Max was too busy laughing and imitating the strange blubbering noise Rufus made as he fled.

"That was amazing!" Max congratulated me.

"Where's Jessica?" I responded.

"Beats me. I guess she took off with everyone else."

"Took off?" I felt like crying. "Why would she do that?"

"Did you see what you looked like?" Max laughed.

"So? I wasn't after anyone but Rufus. And it's not like I was actually going to do anything to him."

"You couldn't tell that from where the rest of us were standing."

I started to walk off.

"Where are you going?" Max called after me.

"To find Jessica." But a hand fell on my shoulder and stopped me dead in my tracks.

"Mizterrr Finkelztein!" I looked up at Parkman's own bowling ball of terror, Principal Walrus W. Weaselman.

"Yes?" I quavered.

"My offize," he ordered. "Now!"

There was no question about it. I was dead. I was about to become the latest addition to the collection of horror stories about the Weasel-man. He opened the door of his office and ushered me in. I took a deep breath and stepped into my worst nightmare.

I nervously glanced around the room. There was no guillotine, no iron maiden, no chains, no eye-gouger, and no hobbling mallet. In fact, there was nothing terrifyingly out of the ordinary at all. The Weasel-man's office looked like any principal's office. Still, I wasn't prepared for what came next. Principal Weaselman told me he didn't care at all about Rufus and the incident with the clown.

"In fact," he confided, "I think Rrrufuz Delaney iz a deplorable little snot who doezn't dezerve to be called a perzon." He then did something that legend claimed he was incapable of. He laughed. Granted, it was the most diabolical thing I've ever

heard in my life, like a chorus of screeching banshees from hell, and his lipless mouth didn't even crack open for a split second, but it still qualified as a laugh.

In my careful effort to not offend this legendary punisher of innocent children, I laughed too. It was a good call. The Weasel-man laughed harder.

It was like we were buddies all of a sudden. He even gave me a pack of gum he'd confiscated from some other kid the day before. "Chew it," he urged me. "Pleaze. Chew it in clazz if you vant. Chew it even though you didn't bring enough for everyone elze. Vat do I carrre, my rrround little friend? You do vateverrr you vant, Mizterrr Finkelztein."

"Wow," I thought. "Why have I spent my entire life avoiding this place?" Everything everyone always said about the Weasel-man was a bunch of garbage. "I love this guy!"

"And what about that Rrronnie Rrrothman?" Principal Weaselman chuckled in his frightening way. "He'z a futurelez lozerrr, too, if I've everrr seen one. Yez no?"

"Yes." I nodded.

For the next half hour, Principal Weaselman gossiped about all the kids he hated at my school. He was so eager to point out every single thing that irritated him that I didn't get a word in the whole time. And then, for no particular reason that I could see, he stopped dissing the other kids, sat up straight, and adjusted his dark gray suit jacket as if he was ready to talk business.

"So." He leaned over his desk. "Iz it true what I heard some of the otherrrz say? Can you rrreally eat a meatball and become anything you vant?"

There was no point in denying it. Every kid in

the hallway had seen me do it. So I told the Weasel-man about the power.

"I muzt see this for myzelf." The principal's mouth was watering. "Hmm, let uz see, what forrr you to do, what forrr you to do? I know. Can you turn yourzelf into that wretched creature Rrrufuz Delaney?"

A meatball later, I was gone, and Rufus Delaney was dancing around the principal's office crying about the killer clown that had tried to hug him to death. When I turned back into Meatball two minutes and thirty-nine seconds later, Principal Weaselman was laughing so hard, he actually started to cry.

"You are the funniezt kid I have everrr met," he praised me. "And this powerrr of yourrrs, it'z truly amazing. You have morrre meatballz, yez no?"

I looked in my backpack. "Only one left."

"Very good. Show me yourrr power one more time, yez no?"

"Sure," I said.

"This time, I vant you to become something that doez not exizt anymorrre." It even seemed like a pointed request at the time, but what did I care? I was on the Weasel-man's good side. "I vant you to become this."

Principal Weaselman handed me a book opened to a drawing labeled "The Extinct Dodo Bird." I popped in my last meatball, and for the next two minutes and thirty-nine seconds, the dodo lived again.

I clucked and cooed about until Principal Weaselman picked me up with both hands and held me to the light. He closely examined me, as if to make sure that his eyes weren't deceiving him and that I wasn't tricking him with smoke and mirrors. Then he grabbed hold of one of the decorative feathers on the top of my head and yanked it out. No longer interested in me, he released me to dodo about the office while he admired the feather taken from my head.

"Ouch." I reappeared, rubbing the top of my head. All my hair seemed to be there, though there was also a welt that *hadn't* been there when I entered the principal's office. "Well"—I zipped up my backpack—"no more meatballs."

The principal wasn't listening. He was preoccupied. Though the dodo was gone, its feather remained. The Weasel-man's face was glowing, and a smile crept across it, eventually becoming so wide that I actually saw the inside of his mouth. He held up the dodo feather. "Fazinating! Yez no?"

"What?" I asked, not sure if I was supposed to

be fascinated with the feather or with my principal's toothless mouth.

"Mizterrr Finkelztein, I like you. I vant to help you."

"Help me what?"

He opened a cabinet labeled PERMANENT RECORDS and pulled out a file with MEATBALL FINKELSTEIN typed on its face. "Let'z be frank." The principal flipped through my record. "You aren't the bezt student. Actually, yourrr gradez are az *kaput* az they can be."

I started to mumble an excuse, but the Weaselman let me off the hook. "Don't torture yourzelf," he comforted me, "I understand. A boy like you haz many diztractions. This iz why pencilz have erazers."

"What are you saying?" I was intrigued.

"What I'm saying iz, let me help you improve yourrr permanent rrrecord. And in exchange, you vill help me."

"How?"

"By partizipating in a superrr-secret extra-credit project. Yez no?"

"I don't know." I squirmed. The thought of having to actually do work to improve my grades wasn't that exciting. "What do I have to do?"

"Starting tomorrow, rrreport to my offizz every

day afterrr school from, let'z say, three to five, eat a few meatballz and become a few thingz. Eazy vork forrr you, and a great help to me."

"How much extra credit do I get?" I wasn't trying to be greedy, but three to five is prime goofing-off time. I needed to make sure that the Weasel-man wasn't just going to change some C I got three years ago to a C+.

"Don't vorry about it," Principal Weaselman assured me. He reached back into the permanent record cabinet and pulled out another file. "You'll get morrre extra credit than any kid haz everrr rrreceived in the hiztory of schoolz. You'll get so much extra credit, you'll have the bezt permanent rrrecord at Parkman. Yourrr gradez will even be betterrr than . . ." He tossed the file in his hand across his desk so I could see its label, which read PRECIOUS FINKELSTEIN.

What could I say to that but "Deal!"

By the time I got out of the Weasel-man's office, first period was long over. Since English is the only class we have together, I didn't see Jessica again all day. I was hoping to catch her at lunch, but she never showed up.

"She's avoiding me. Isn't she, Max?"

"Yes," Max admitted. "But the good news is, so is everyone else."

Max was right. Not only was no one sitting at our table, no one was sitting at any of the tables around us, which didn't stop anyone from staring at me. Max waved across the cafeteria, and everyone immediately diverted their eyes, like they were glancing around the room instead of looking at me.

"Has anyone seen Rufus?" I asked.

"Beats me. Why?"

"Just curious. Do you think I overdid it this morning?"

"Please." Max laughed. "He had it coming."

"I guess he did."

"Cheer up, Meatball. You have a super power, remember? Idiots like Rufus Delaney are never going to bother you again."

"I know, I know, that's great. Really. It's just . . . ah, forget it."

"Why don't you call her after school?" Max advised.

"Is that what you'd do?"

Max just looked at me. I don't know why I asked

him that. Outside the one time he exploded in Precious's face, Max has never spoken to a girl, you know, in that way. It's strange—as fine as he is about only having one arm when it comes to anything else, Max has convinced himself that no girl would ever want to date him because of it.

"Sorry, Max. You're right, I should call her."

And that's what I did. When I got home after school, I marched straight into my room, gathered all my courage, and called Jessica at home. Unfortunately, her father was waiting to cut me off at the pass.

"Oh, h-hi," I stammered. "Can I speak with Jessica, please?"

"Can I ask who's calling?"

"Meatball Finkelstein, sir."

"I'm sorry, Meatball, but Jessica asked me to tell you she's not home."

"Dad!" I heard Jessica yell at him through the phone.

"What?" her dad asked.

"She's not home?" I challenged.

"That's right, son, she's not home." Her dad was attempting, in a typical parentally lame sort of way, to cover up his blunder. "But it has nothing to do with how you scared her this morning."

"Dad!" I heard Jessica yell again.

"Have a nice night, Meatball," Jessica's dad said as he hung up the phone.

I tried calling her about a hundred more times that afternoon. Okay, so I didn't actually dial her complete number again for several hours, but I did pick up the phone several hundred times and dial a few of her numbers. Then, around six o'clock, I finally forced myself to dial the whole thing. Her line was busy: Either the phone was off the hook or she was talking to her high school boyfriend, not that I had any evidence that she had a high school boyfriend.

I knew what I had to do. "I'm going over there!" I grabbed my jacket, marched down the hall, and opened the front door at the exact moment Mom and Dad were walking in with dinner.

"Oh, good," my mom said when she saw me, and she handed me a grocery bag from our market, turned me around, and told me to put it in the kitchen for her. I pushed through the kitchen door to put the bag on the table, like I always do, but the table was gone, as were the chairs, the blender, the food processor, and the dishwasher.

I turned back to my dad and asked, "Where is everything?"

"We'll talk about it over dinner, buddy," my dad said with a grimace, and he patted me on the shoulder. "I have to go change, so do me a favor and set the"—he looked at the spot where the kitchen table had once stood—"floor."

When my dad took a seat on the floor between me and my mom, he let out an achey moan, and I looked at him. I really looked at both of my parents, for the first time in as long as I could remember. Their eyes were lost in puffy pink rings, their hair needed some serious combing, and their cheeks drooped below their jawbones. They looked terrible.

Dad stretched his arms above his head, yawned really big, and said, "So, Meatball, Precious—your mom and I want to talk to you two about the changes going on around here."

"You know, kids . . ." My mom took her turn in what I could already tell was a well-scripted performance. "Sometimes things don't work out the way parents mean them to."

"Exactly." My dad jumped back in. "And this is one of those times." He took a deep breath. "The

long and the short of it is this: Our business is in trouble. We got hit real bad when Super Health moved in, and, in hindsight, we probably should have closed up shop, cut our losses, and walked away. But we didn't."

"We thought people would get sick of the face-less corporate service," my mom explained, "and that'd they'd come back to the personal, family touch of Tofu For-u. We were wrong."

"What your mom and I are trying to say is, if we don't come up with $37,816.14 in the next three weeks—and let's be honest here, there's no way that's going to happen—the bank is going to take the store."

"Is that what happened to the furniture?" I asked.

"No." My dad forced a smile, though I could see more shame swelling up in the rings around his eyes. "We had to sell the furniture to pay our rent and some other bills."

"Money's going to be tight for a while," my mom conceded. "And we're all going to have to cut back wherever we can, which means"—and she looked at Precious when she said this—"no more lessons for the time being."

"What?" Precious screeched. "This is so unfair! How come I have to make all the sacrifices?"

One of the benefits of not being good at anything was that I really didn't have anything to give up. Or so I thought.

"We're all making sacrifices, Precious." My dad raised his voice a bit.

"Really?" Precious stood up and screamed.

"Yes." My father restrained himself. "For starters, we're going to have to find a new apartment. A smaller one." He looked at my mom.

She took a deep breath and broke the news. "You two will have to share a room."

"I will never share a room with that loser!" Precious cried, and she stormed out of the kitchen.

"I'll go talk to her," my mom said, and she followed my sister out.

"Your sister didn't mean it, buddy." My dad

smiled. "Now, pass me one of those meatless chicken wings, would you?"

"Speaking of chicken, Dad," I said as I passed him the artificial meat, "I wanted to ask you something. What would you do if a teacher offered you tons of extra credit and really good grades, but, in exchange, you had to—"

"Meatball." My dad cut me off. "Whatever it was a teacher asked me to do, I'd do it, because nothing is more important than good grades."

"Nothing?"

"Nothing." My dad nodded and sank his teeth into the phony chicken wing.

I wouldn't exactly say that I came clean with my dad as much as I tricked him into giving me a defense in the event that he and my mom should ever find out that I was eating meat. "What?" I would say. "I didn't want to eat it, I was just doing what I had to to get good grades."

Ah, who was I kidding? They were still going to kill me.

23

After I did the dishes (by hand, since the dish-washer had been sold along with everything else), I told my dad I was going to Max's to work on a school project. Thankfully, my mom, who would have detected the lie before it even came out of my mouth, was still comforting Precious. Once out the door, I hopped in a cab and headed across town to Jessica's.

I wasn't really sure what I wanted to tell her. I mean, I had only met the girl the day before. And though all I wanted to do was talk to her, all she wanted to do was avoid me. So when I rang the doorbell, I didn't know what I was expecting, or what I was hoping to accomplish.

Jessica's father opened the front door, but all I saw was a nose. His large, crooked, twisted nose was easily three times larger than most big-nosed people's noses. I couldn't help but stare at the schnoz. I was under its spell.

"Can I help you?" the nose seemed to ask.

"H-hi," I stammered. "I'm Meatball Finkelstein, we spoke on the phone."

"Right." Mr. George looked me up and down, and I remembered that I was no great package either. I mean, what was I, Meatball Finkelstein, doing critiquing someone else's *uniqueness,* as my mom calls it? "Jessica told me all about you."

"Did she use the word 'fat'?" I wondered to myself, though I kept my mouth shut.

"She's not home." Mr. George shrugged.

"Oh," I said, clearly not buying it.

"Really." Jessica's dad shrugged again. "She's at a piano lesson." He smiled at me and said, "And I'm not lying this time."

"Oh well," I said, deflated, "can you tell her I stopped by?"

"Sure will." Her dad smiled. "Have a nice night, Meatball."

I turned around and huffed off. I guess I must have looked as pathetic as I felt because halfway between Jessica's apartment and the elevators, her father yelled, "Hey, Meatball."

I turned back.

"You all right?"

I avoided the question with a strange guttural "Eh"-type noise.

"Why don't you come in for a minute?" Mr. George suggested. "We can talk." He smiled and added, "I just made some cookies."

"Was that a fat comment?"
I asked myself.

"Who cares?" I answered on behalf of my stomach. "The important thing is that you find out what kind of cookies he's talking about."

So I followed Mr. George into his apartment. I'm glad I did, because Jessica's dad turned out to be a good guy and an even better baker.

Mr. George handed me a cookie, a glass of milk, and the truth. "Jessica's scared of you, Meatball."

"Why?"

"The way you dealt with the Rufus kid, is that his name?"

I nodded.

"It frightened her. What did you do, anyway?"

"I sort of exploded, I guess you could say. But he had it coming. He's been torturing me since the first grade."

"Why?"

"Because I'm fat, and because I'm named Meatball, and because I'm a vegetarian, and because he's a jerk. So she hates me, huh?"

"Let me ask you something, Meatball. You like Jessica, right?"

"Yes, sir."

"Why?"

"I just do."

"How do you know?"

"Well, every time I'm around her I want to puke."

"Fair enough." Mr. George laughed.

"She's amazing, Mr. George. Whatever you and Jessica's mom are doing, keep it up."

"Actually, Jessica's mom passed away years ago."

"Oh." I felt like a bigger donkey than Rufus. "I'm sorry."

"Don't worry about it. You were saying?"

"I don't get Jessica. She doesn't care about my name, she doesn't care what I look like, she doesn't care that my friend Max only has one arm. It's like she can see past all the stuff that everyone else hates about us and . . ." I stopped myself. I was literally staring the answer to my question in the face. Well, in the nose. In that instant, it all became clear, and Jessica's father's nose shrank before my eyes.

For the first time, I noticed his pleasant green eyes (just like the eyes I adored so much in Jessica) and his well-trimmed brown hair and his warm smile. The nose was gone, and all I could see was kindness—only a fraction of what Jessica saw when she looked at him, I'm sure.

"You okay, Meatball?" Mr. George asked.

"Fine." Then I asked, "Does she hate me now?"

"Not at all. If I'm not mistaken, I'd say she's rather fond of you. Meatball, you have to understand that Jessica's been through a lot. A month ago she was living in a house by the beach in Santa Monica, California, walking distance from every friend she had in the world. This week she's in New York City, and the only person she knows is her dad."

I cringed, because if there's one thing I have plenty of, it's compassion for a kid in a difficult situation.

"You're a good guy, Meatball Finkelstein. Don't give up on my Jessica just yet. Deal?"

"Deal."

We shook on it, and Mr. George gave me an extra cookie for the taxi ride home. By the way, they were oatmeal chocolate chip.

For the next few days, I didn't see Jessica once outside of English class. I couldn't speak to her in class because she got Nizami Pastrami's permission to swap seats with Ronnie Rothman, and by the time I made it into the hallway after the bell rang, she was gone. Though I would have liked to stop by her apartment again, I had no time. I had to report to the Weasel-man's office at three every afternoon to work on the super-secret extra-credit project.

Principal Weaselman kept me working until five every evening, at which point he'd dismiss me with the same reminder. "Thiz iz a superrr-secret project, and you muzt speak of it to no one." By five-fifteen I'd be at Max's, telling him every single detail.

The problem was that the project was so secret, I didn't even know what I was doing. All I knew was that I was helping the Weasel-man concoct something called Formula FV. I didn't know what it was, what it was for, or why I was making it, though not for lack of asking.

Every day, I'd say, "What is Formula FV, anyway?"

To which Principal Weaselman would respond, "In due time, Mizterrr Finkelztein, in due time."

So I'd ask, "What's Formula FV for?"

And Principal Weaselman would answer, "In due time, Mizterrr Finkelztein, in due time."

"Well, why am I making Formula FV?"

"In due time, Mizterrr Finkelztein, in due time."

"Whatever it is," I thought, "When I'm done with this project, I better have the best grades in the school, because making FV hurts. A lot."

When I showed up at the principal's office on

the first afternoon, there was a plate of meatballs sitting on his desk. Beside the plate, Principal Weaselman had laid out several tools, including a large pair of nail clippers; a selection of saws, chisels, and hammers; gardener's shears; dental pliers; and the biggest carrot peeler I had ever seen. A clear pitcher the size of a hefty garbage can sat next to the various tools. The pitcher was labeled FORMULA FV and was partially filled with a green, gooey substance, not dissimilar to phlegm. The dodo feather that the principal had torn off my head the day before floated on top of the green goop.

Principal Weaselman rolled up his sleeves, put on a butcher's apron and goggles, and asked, "Are you rrready to begin?"

"I guess so. What are all those tools for?"

"In due time, Mizterrr Finkelztein," the principal answered, "in due time." He locked the door,

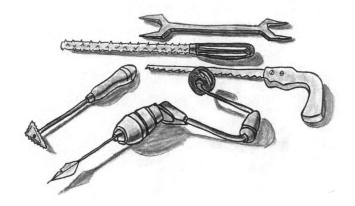

handed me a meatball, and showed me a picture of a pterodactyl.

The moment I turned into the prehistoric creature, Principal Weaselman grabbed the oversized nail clippers, put in some earplugs, and went to work on my biggest toenail. He was cutting the nail off right where it emerged from the skin, which hurt like when I cut one of my own nails too short, only a hundred thousand times worse. I screamed in pain, creating a mind-numbing screeching sound that hasn't been heard on this planet in millions of years. Protected by his earplugs, the principal concentrated on the giant nail. Seconds before I turned back into Meatball, it came off.

Eager to continue, the principal handed me another meatball. I couldn't do it, though. My foot hurt way too much. It felt like someone had attacked it with a Weedwacker. I ripped my shoe and sock off to see the damage. My toenail was still there. It was just blacker and bluer than it used to be, and it was throbbing like crazy. Principal Weaselman dropped the pterodactyl nail into the pitcher on his desk.

"All great achievements come from the blood, sweat, and pain of equally great people. Great people like you, Mizterrr Finkelztein. Ve vill proceed veneverrr you are rrready. Take az much time az you need."

Half an hour later, the pain passed. I grabbed a meatball and swallowed it as if I had been eating beef my whole life. The Weasel-man showed me a picture of a Sala Sala tree. A caption beneath the photograph of the exotic orange-and-violet tree explained that the Sala Sala only grew in a section of the Amazon that was slashed and burned thirty years earlier by some humongous corporation. Two minutes and thirty-nine seconds gave the principal and his gardener's shears more than enough time to cut off several Sala Sala branches, Sala Sala flowers, Sala Sala leaves, and a strip of extinct Sala Sala bark. By the time I turned back into Meatball, I felt like I had been skinned alive. While Principal Weaselman added the Sala Sala flowers, leaves, branches, and bark to his mystery formula, I lay down on the couch and zonked out.

I woke up at ten to five, and, though my skin was red and irritated, the pain was gone, more or less—well, less. Unfortunately, the Weasel-man was still there, standing over me with another meatball. "One more and ve call it a day, yez no?"

"Maybe we can call it a day now," I suggested. "Can we pick it up here tomorrow?"

"No." The principal smiled. "It'z bezt that ve finish today'z vork today. Othervize, maybe yourrr gradez get betterrr, but not so much. That vould be a shame, yez no?"

"Sure would," I mumbled. I inspected the next image and gulped down another meatball.

"A Sellian Gigantus Coral formation?" I thought as I became the enormous rock found only on the deepest, most hard-to-reach parts of the ocean's floor.

"What can he do to a rock?" I wondered.

"Nothing that hurts," I assured myself.

The principal smashed a chisel into the Sellian Gigantus (which happened to be me!), and he didn't stop pounding until a baseball-sized chunk came loose. When I became myself again, I was ready to go home, eat some dinner, go to sleep, and never return to the Weaselman's office.

There was a note on the refrigerator from my mom.

Kids,

Your dad and I aren't going to be home until late tonight. There's a veggie lasagna in the fridge for dinner.

Love, Mom

"Perfect," I thought, "I can grab some food and go to sleep without talking to anyone."

But when I opened the fridge, all I could find was the carcass of a lasagna. This had Precious written all over it. Whatever she had not eaten was covered in orange juice from the container on the shelf above that must have *accidentally* fallen over. Too tired to care, I trudged to my room to lie down and sleep, only to discover that my bed, along with my desk, dresser, and other furniture, was gone.

I rummaged through a pile in my closet, pulled out a sleeping bag, and crawled inside. According to my alarm clock, which had been tossed on the floor by whoever took my bedside table, it was only six-twenty-eight, but I didn't care. I closed my eyes and went to sleep.

As I walked down the hallway toward my locker on Thursday morning, the sea of students parted before me. Since Tuesday, the other kids had stopped speaking when I walked by and started averting their eyes until I passed. Then they stared at my back. I couldn't see them, I just felt them.

Many if not all of my classmates told their parents about the kid who'd eaten a meatball and shape-shifted before their eyes. Fortunately for me, most parents don't believe their kids when they make wild claims, regardless of whether they're true or false.

The few parents who gave their children the benefit of the doubt called the principal's office, only to receive a scolding from the Weasel-man. "Don't vaste my valuable time vith yourrr stupid child'z anticz," he squealed at each caller as he hung up on them. Either way, no one was calling my mom and dad. Lost in their own problems, they still had no idea that I had eaten a single meatball, let alone that I was spending my afternoons downing them like they were grapes— horrible, rancid grapes. I wondered if I'd ever get used to eating meat.

Max was waiting by my locker.

"Whoa," he greeted me. "You look awful."

"Thanks." I opened my locker, wishing I could crawl inside and go back to sleep.

"This is kind of nice." Max gestured down the hall at my nervous schoolmates. "Isn't it?"

"Yeah," I admitted. The truth was, I liked being feared a lot more than being hated.

"No more sessions, either."

"Anyone seen Rufus yet?" Rufus Delaney hadn't been back to school since his encounter with the clown.

"Not yet." Max smiled.

That Thursday seemed to last forever. All morning, I waited for lunch period, and when Jessica didn't show up in the cafeteria, I spent all afternoon waiting for English, which I had last period that day. As soon as the bell rang, I ran out into the hallway to catch Jessica. She slipped into the crowd, and I dove in after her. Just ahead of me, I could see her break left toward the side doors. I followed, and as I opened the doors, a familiar squeal halted me. "Mizterrr Finkelztein, you haven't forgotten ourrr deal, have you?" I watched Jessica get into a taxi.

With the previous day's pain far behind me and the carrot of better grades than Precious's dangling in front of me, I returned to the principal's office. Thursday turned out to hurt more than Wednesday. First I became a saber-toothed tiger and the Weasel-man pulled out both my saber-teeth. Then I became a woolly mammoth and he removed a large portion of my furry pelt. After he shaved off several pieces of my unicorn's horn with his medieval-looking oversized carrot peeler, he snipped the fins off the merman I knew I shouldn't have become and plucked the eyelashes out of my gargantuan cyclops eye.

As I crawled out of his office that evening, past the nearly full FV pitcher, the Weasel-man tried to cheer me up. "There are only two metamorphosez left tomorrow. You'll be done vith all this superrr-secret extra credit beforrre you know it." Easy words coming from the man who gets to inflict the pain.

After I was released from Principal Weaselman's chamber of tortures, I limped over to Max's.

"You have to do me a huge favor, Max."

"What's up?"

"After school tomorrow, go over to Jessica's and give her this note. I would do it myself, but that might get in the way of the incredible amounts of pain the Weasel-man has planned for me."

"All right." It was no skin off good old reliable Max's back. "Whatever you need, Meatball."

"Thank you," I sighed. Max would handle the situation much better than I ever could. "One thing though," I added. "No matter what, don't tell her anything about the super-secret extra-credit project."

And so, the next afternoon, while I was in the principal's office, Max went over to Jessica's and told her all about the super-secret extra-credit project I was doing.

The way Max explained it to me later was that

Jessica instantly forgot about how I frightened her because she was concerned for me.

"That means she likes me, right?" I asked, but Max didn't know for sure. According to Max, their conversation went something like this:

"Something's not right," Jessica told Max. "I've only been at Parkman for a few days and I already know that the Weasel-man is a jerk. He's mean. Really mean. Actually, he's the meanest, grumpiest, most disagreeable person I've ever met in my life. You said it yourself in the cafeteria the other day. He hates kids. I don't even know why he ever became a principal to begin with."

"Meatball thinks it's because it's the only job that will let him legally torture us."

"Okay, so why's he being so nice to one of us?"

"Why?" Max shrugged, stumped.

"I don't know." Jessica was equally stumped. "I think Meatball's in trouble."

"Oh," Max said, remembering. "Meatball wanted me to give you this."

He handed her my note.

I'm sorry I scared you. Just tell me what to do to get you to talk to me again.

Meatball

Meanwhile, in the principal's office, I, of course, had no idea what was going on at Jessica's house. All I knew was that when a legendary wallezigator has a tentacle plucked off its back with a pair of hydraulic tweezers, it doesn't feel good. While I recovered, Principal Weaselman excused himself to attend his Friday-afternoon PTA meeting.

"I'll be back in thirty minutez, and then this vill all be overrr forrr you."

I lay down on the couch, closed my eyes, and waited for the pain that was shooting up, down, and all over my bruised back to go away.

"Meatball, wake up."

"I'm not sleeping, Max," I muttered, annoyed. "And when I open my eyes, you'd better not be here."

But when I opened my eyes, not only was Max standing beside me in the principal's office, Jessica was with him.

"What are you doing here?" I demanded. "Do

you know how much trouble I could get in? And thanks so much for not saying anything to Jessica. Hi, Jessica," I sheepishly muttered.

"Hi." She kind of waved. Then she smiled, and I could see that she had forgiven me for everything.

So I smiled back at her and said, "Get out of here!"

"Okay, but you have to come with us."

"I can't. I have to finish something here."

"Meatball." Max jumped in. "Jessica thinks you're in trouble, and I think she might be right."

"I'm not in trouble. Yet. But I will be if you two don't leave before the Weasel-man comes back."

"Of course you're in trouble," Jessica insisted. "Do you think the Weasel-man gave you this extra-credit project because he suddenly cares about how well you do in school?"

"Well . . ." I tried to answer.

"What?" Jessica challenged me.

"Look, I've been working my butt off, and I've been through a lot of pain, and now I'm one meat-ball away from the payoff. And I'm not stupid, thank you very much, I know the Weasel-man isn't helping me out just to be nice."

"Then why is he helping you?" Jessica asked.

"Because I'm helping him make his Formula FV."

"Do you even know what that is?" Jessica demanded.

"Yes," I said, defending myself. "It's the secret formula that gives me good grades and makes my parents proud of me instead of my sister, for once."

Max and Jessica both glared at me.

"What?" I asked.

"Nothing," they both said.

"Well, then, leave. Please."

But they didn't have a chance, because the next thing any of us heard was the sound of Principal Weaselman walking back to his office. I pushed Max and Jessica behind the couch, and just as they hit the ground, the Weasel-man returned. "All rrrecovered, I azume?"

"Rrready when you arrre," I joked.

"Very good." The principal grimaced. He handed me a meatball and a picture. "The dodecapuss," the small caption beneath the drawing read, "is a mythical twelve-armed creature who rules the seas." It took the principal nearly all of the two minutes and thirty-nine seconds to remove my slimy blue dodecapuss tongue, but, as always, he got it in the end. The Weasel-man dropped the jiggly tongue into his Formula FV pitcher, and my job was done.

"Mizterrr Finkelztein, you have done exzellent vork." I checked my mouth to make sure I still had my tongue. I did, though my gums were bleeding pretty badly. "I'm so delighted vith you that not only am I going to upgrade yourrr pazt markz to A'z, I am going to give you straight A'z on all futurrre vorks. That iz, juzt az long az no one everrr hearrrz about what ve have done herrre this veek."

"No problem," I grunted, just happy to be done and in one piece. "You don't mind if I take a meatball for the road," I asked, exhausted, "do you?"

"Be my guezt."

I grabbed a meatball and took off. After I was out of the Weasel-man's sight, I downed the meatball and thought "Invisible." Two minutes and thirty-nine seconds later, I reappeared behind the principal's couch, Max on one side of me, Jessica on the other.

"Straight A's," I quietly boasted. "I told you I wasn't in any trouble."

27

Everybody knows what the PTA is, right? It's the Parent-Teacher Association. There's one for every school in the entire world. So when Principal Weaselman logged on to the Internet and video-linked with the president of the Parkman PTA, a woman named Mrs. Delaney (as in Rufus Delaney's mom), we didn't think it was too strange. Okay, it was a little odd that Mrs. Delaney and the principal communicated via televideo technology, but Parkman's a really nice school.

Remarkably, it seemed as though Mrs. Delaney saluted our principal when she first saw him, but it was hard to tell from behind the sofa. Fortunately, we could hear just fine. "Principal Principal . . ." Mrs. Delaney seemed to stammer when she greeted the Weasel-man. "Good evening."

"Prezident Delaney," the principal responded, his back to us, "I have excellent newz. After yearrrz and yearrrz and yearrrz of failurrrez, Formula FV iz one push of a button away from exziztenze! Az alwayz, my word haz come to pass."

The principal picked up the enormous pitcher that was filled with all the things that he had cut, pried, prodded, pulled, and ripped off me over the course of the week. He covered it with a rubber lid and stuck it onto a base, which he wheeled out from underneath his desk. The enormous pitcher was part of an enormous blender!

Principal Weaselman took a deep breath. He seemed to be relishing the moment, while Mrs. Delaney looked on from the computer screen with a devilish smile. Then the principal switched on the blender. It stirred, mixed, chopped, shook, crushed, ground, puréed, pulverized, and liquefied the ingredients until all that remained was a clear green gel.

"Finally," the principal said, his body inflating with pride, "ve have the FV!"

"Congratulations, Principal Principal," Mrs. Delaney said, stammering again. "This is truly a magnificent day."

They were both so happy about the FV that I turned to Max and Jessica and boasted again, "See? I'm the one who *finally* made the FV. Me! Cool, huh?"

Max and Jessica ignored me and stayed focused on the principal. He poured the contents of the pitcher into an empty two-liter soda bottle that he pulled out of one of his desk drawers.

When the last drop had been transferred, the principal looked back at his monitor. "Rrready the PTAz of the vorld," he hissed. "Formula FV vill be diztributed to every boy and every girrrl on the globe by next veek's end. Soon they vill all be vishing they were neverrr born!"

My stomach turned.

"Yes, sir," Mrs. Delaney barked. She raised her hand to her forehead again, and this time there was no mistaking it. She was saluting our principal. "Congratulations once again, Principal Principal." Her image disappeared from the monitor.

I looked at Jessica and Max. "What is the FV?" I mouthed.

They shook their heads at me, but they couldn't speak. We were afraid to move or even breathe. We had no choice but to stay put.

The principal video-linked with a man who was wearing a dark gray suit and dark gray tie just like Principal Weaselman always wore. The only difference in their suits was that the man on the computer monitor had a gold number 2 stitched onto his lapel.

"Principal Principal," the number two man said with a smart salute "I have everyone on standby. The PWO awaits your instructions."

"Very good, Secondary Prinzipal. I'm on my vay down." The computer screen went dark, and the

Weasel-man clicked his heels together, turned around, and marched out of his office.

Once we heard the door lock, and we were sure he was gone, we stood up and stretched. "Um," I sort of gulped, "so, what do you guys think I made?"

"Beats me." Max shrugged.

My stomach was churning away at full steam. Any pride I had felt in my super-secret extra-credit work had vanished. All that remained was a lump of eerily nauseating suspicion.

"Whatever it is," Jessica weighed in, "it's not good."

"I agree with that." Max nodded.

"Do either of you happen to know what the PWO is?" I asked.

They shook their heads no.

"Do you know why everyone keeps saying 'Principal' twice?"

They shook their heads no, again.

"Do you know why everything is abbreviated?"

They shook their heads no, again.

"We should go home now, shouldn't we?"

They shook their heads no, again.

"We should follow him?" I asked, despite myself.

They nodded their heads yes, despite themselves.

We trailed Principal Weaselman as he turned the corner at the far end of the hallway. When I glanced around the corner, he was already gone. The good and bad news was that there was only one door in the short, dead-end hallway. To follow our principal, we had to go where no student had gone before. We had to enter the faculty lounge.

I nudged the door open. The lounge seemed empty. I looked at Max and Jessica, and together we entered the forbidden lair.

Talk about your letdowns. Where were the soda fountains, the video games, the state-of-the-art computers, the robot butlers? The faculty lounge looked just like any other room in the school. It had the same cardboard carpet and the same dirty paint. The only differences were that it had chairs and tables where the other rooms had desks, and it had bad art where the others had blackboards.

"Where did he go?" Max asked.

Jessica looked at me.

I shrugged.

The bathroom door creaked open.

We all froze in place.

"Is he in there?" Max mumbled under his breath.

"I don't hear anything," I whispered.

"And the lights are out," Jessica noted.

"And," I added, pointing to the sign on the wall, "it's out of order."

"So," Max wondered aloud, a little freaked, "why'd the door just open?"

It was definitely a good question. I unfroze long enough to yank the bathroom door open all the way.

"You can open your eyes." Jessica giggled. Embarrassed, I unsquinted and looked. Aside from the toilet and the sink, the dark bathroom was empty.

"Now what?" Max asked.

"He must have gone in here, right? I mean, there's no other choice," I pointed out.

Max, Jessica, and I crowded into the rest room to look around. There were no other entrances or exits and no windows. I leaned up against one of the walls. Grimy slime crept off the filthy bathroom wall onto my hand.

"Ewww," I groaned, "gross."

I squeezed between Max and Jessica to get to the sink and tried the hot water, but none came out. So I tried the cold water, and immediately my stomach lurched as the three of us plummeted down beneath the school. The whole bathroom— sink, toilet, dirty walls, and all—was dropping with us. We weren't in an out-of-order bathroom, we were in an *in*-order elevator.

The bathroom-elevator abruptly stopped and we stepped out into a poorly lit hallway several stories below our school. The elevator door closed behind us, and the phony bathroom returned to the faculty lounge above. The dank hallway smelled like chalk dust and toner cartridges. The air was wet and thick, and we could barely see ten feet in front of us. We could, however, hear the principal's shoes hastily *du-dump*ing along up ahead.

"Maybe we shouldn't be doing this." Max was overcome with a wave of rationality. "Let's go back," he said. There was a call button for the elevator on one of the damp walls. "I think we're in over our heads."

Jessica, originally the voice of nosiness and suspicion, now agreed with Max. "Yeah, come on, Meatball."

"You guys go," I offered, and I hit the button to call the bathroom-elevator back.

"What are you going to do?" Jessica asked.

"I'm going to keep following the Weasel-man."

"Bad idea," Max warned.

"Yeah," Jessica agreed, "there's nothing but serious trouble at the end of this hallway."

"I know." I grimaced. The elevator arrived. "And to tell the truth, I don't want to go down there. I'm a wimp."

"A total wimp." Max backed me up.

"Thanks, buddy."

Max smiled.

"But you heard what the Weasel-man said.

When the PTA distributes that FV, every boy and girl in the world will wish they had never been born. Seeing how I'm the one who made it, I kind of feel obligated to stop him."

"How?" Max asked.

I shrugged. "I'll be careful," I told my friends. "I promise."

"I'm staying too." Max looked at Jessica, who nodded. "I hope we don't regret this." He reached into the bathroom-elevator and turned the cold water faucet on. It returned upstairs, empty.

We followed the hall as it curved to the left, to the right, and back to the left. We turned several corners, went up and down a few molehills, and headed around one last bend until we could see the final fifty-foot stretch of hallway ahead of us. We could barely make out the shape of Principal Weaselman standing at the far end of the hallway. Two thick metal doors slowly creaked open in front of him and light poured out into the hallway. We stepped back to hide in the shadows and watch.

The man with the gold number 2 stitched onto his lapel—the secondary principal, as the Weaselman had called him—stepped into the hallway and saluted. "Principal Principal. We've already coordinated with our friends in the PTA. The arrangements for distribution of the FV are under way."

"Brrrilliant!" Principal Weaselman squeaked. "Today vill go down in hiztory az the day the PWO made good on its commitment to honorrr its PPP."

"What's with all the letters?" Max asked. Jessica and I shrugged.

The secondary principal led the Weasel-man, or the principal principal, as people seemed to be calling him now, into the room at the end of the hallway. The massive doors closed behind the two men, and the hallway was dark again.

When we thought it was safe, we scurried down the hall. As we approached the ominous doors, we saw that a picture of a weeping child in chains was engraved into the face of the double doors. It was the same image that decorated the ring the Weasel-man wore around his thumb. Only, on the doors, three words were carved in colossal block letters above the crying kid:

PRINCIPALS' WORLD ORDER

30

The answers to all our questions waited on the other side of the massive PWO doors.

"There's no way we're going to barge in there," I bravely blurted out.

"No, really?" Jessica mocked.

"Thanks for the bulletin," Max added.

Clearly, we were going to have to find answers somewhere else. Entering the PWO headquarters would be a suicide mission, which is why we headed back to the Weasel-man's office instead.

Jessica searched the principal's computer, I rummaged through his desk drawers, and Max kept a lookout. The computer only offered cafeteria schedules, holiday information, grades, and other useless info. The desk drawers contained even less.

"Here's what we'll do," I suggested. "We'll put everything back the way it was, take the bottle of FV, get out of here, and figure this all out later. The Weasel-man can't do anything without the FV, right?"

"I guess." Jessica shrugged. "It'd be easier to answer that if we knew what FV stood for."

"True," I admitted, "but wouldn't you rather

solve that puzzle in the comfort and safety of our own homes?"

"I see your point." Jessica nodded. We both grabbed the Weaselman's stapler at the same time to put it back in his drawer, and, each of us thinking that the other person had it, we both let it go at the same time. It fell into the top drawer, and the bottom of the drawer popped up like a seesaw.

I removed the false bottom. The space between the real bottom and the false bottom was filled with all sorts of PWO papers, photos, and miscellaneous paraphernalia. Sitting right on top of the pile was a computer disc labeled

PWO Annual Meeting Minutes

I ran out and checked on Max, who was happy to report that there was no sign of our principal. Jessica popped the disc into the Weasel-man's computer and an image of the man himself appeared on the screen.

Principal Weaselman stood at a lectern on a stage and addressed a crowd of hundreds of men and women. Everyone in the auditorium wore the same dark gray suit and dark gray tie. And, like the secondary principal, they all had different gold numbers stitched onto their lapels.

"Friendz," Principal Weaselman began, holding

up his hands for silence, "colleagues, behold, the Prinzipal Prinzipal's Prinziple!"

Horns blasted. The crowd rose to their feet. Behind the principal, a velvet curtain parted and revealed a large rolled-up parchment. The principal principal (a.k.a. the Weasel-man) untied the leather strap that bound the scroll and unrolled it for all to see. The Principal Principal's Principle— "The PPP!" Jessica realized—was a simple two-word statement: *Kids Stink!*

The dark-gray-clad crowd of principals stood in quiet awe before their motto. Their silence was soon broken, however, by the sound of one principal clapping. Her colleagues joined her, and the room erupted into a roar of excitement.

"Yez." Principal Weaselman spoke over the clamor of the crowd. "It'z truer today than it waz when ourrr forefatherrrz wrote it generationz ago. Kidz Stink!" he cried out, jubilant.

Again the room exploded.

"And this yearrr, my friendz"—the crowd quieted down to hear its principal principal—"iz the yearrr that ve finally do something about it!"

The crowd burst into another chorus of cheers.

"Overrr the pazt twenty yearrrz," their leader continued, "I have not rrrezted forrr a moment. When I am not punishing putrid little children—az we are all duty-bound to do—I vork on some vay, any vay, to addrez the problem prezented by our PPP. Yez, we all know kidz stink, but what can ve do about it? Earlierrr thiz month, I am pleazed to announze, my vork began to blozzom."

The crowd took a deep breath of anticipation.

"The failurrrez of the pazt vill soon be behind uz. Today, my fellow prinzipals of the PWO, ve begin ourrr march forward into a kidlezz futurrre! When the Prinzipal Prinzipal's Ring of the Chained Child waz bestowed upon me twenty yearrrz ago"—Principal Weaselman held out his thumb for everyone to gaze at his creepy ring—"I vowed action. I vowed that I vould find a vay to honorrr ourrr PPP. Today I give you the map to ourrr succezz. Today I am pleazed to rrreport to you that I have uncovered the exact formula forrr making FV!"

"FV!" The crowd in the room gawked in stunned disbelief.

"I know." Principal Weaselman smiled, never

opening his mouth. "Ve've all been led to believe by prinzipal prinzipalz of the pazt that it vaz impozzible, that the FV vaz lozt to uz. Not so! What vaz once a mythology will soon be a rrreality!"

"How do we get FV?" one of the eager principals in the audience screamed.

"In due time," the principal answered, "my dearrr prinzipalz, in due time."

"Tell it to us now," one principal called out.

"Yeah!" another screamed.

"Silenz!" barked the principal principal, and the room instantly became quiet. "Do you forget where you are? Do you forget who I am? I am the prinzipal prinzipal! This iz unaczeptable!"

The crowd of principals quivered like scared kids.

"That's better! Now, where vaz I? Oh, yez. I have made the formula forrr the Fun Vaczine!"

The room exploded in applause again.

"Fun Vaccine?" Jessica asked me.

"FV," I said, hazarding a guess.

"As you know"—the principal principal was glowing with pride—"one drop of FV iz enough to turn every child in a single town into an adult. And, of courze, the effect iz one hundred perzent irrrrreverrrzible."

"Incredible!" someone hollered.

"Magnificent!"

"Stupendible!"

"Izn't it?" the principal principal asked. "Imagine, if one drop eliminatez fun from one town, a single two-literrr bottle filled with FV vould be more than enough to turn every boy and every girrrl in the vorld into an adult. Vith the azzizztanze of ourrr alliez in the PTA, it vould take uz lezz than a veek to rrrid ourrr vorld of children."

"Guys!" Max ran in as the crowd of principals burst into another chorus of loud cheers. "He's coming!"

Jessica yanked the disc out of the computer and dropped it in the drawer. I replaced the false bottom, pushed everything else back in, and slammed the drawer.

"How are we going to get out of here?" Max said, panicky.

"The window," I suggested.

"We're on the second floor," Jessica pointed out.

"Just open it. And, Max, hold this." I handed him the soda bottle filled with FV. "Whatever you do, don't open it, don't touch it, and don't let go of it."

I grabbed one of the leftover meatballs on the Weasel-man's desk, looked out the window, and conjured up an image of myself flying. I shoved the meatball down my throat, and wings unfurled from my arms. Moments before the principal wandered back into his office, a pigeon big enough to fly in Macy's Thanksgiving Day Parade took off out the window with Jessica and Max hanging on for their lives.

As we flew to safety, I caught a quick glimpse through a window of the apartment building across the street from our school, where Rufus Delaney happens to live. Rufus was curled up on his bed, wearing footsie pajamas, gripping his teddy with one hand and sucking the thumb on the other.

31

After I dropped Max and Jessica safely on the ground, we split up for the night. Jessica went to her home, Max went to his, and I took the FV straight over to Gramps's. It was the first time I had been to his apartment since I'd turned into an elephant and destroyed the place. I sat down at the new kitchen table, pushed aside his deck of cards, and told him everything. I told him about the super-secret extra-credit project, about what Max, Jessica, and I had seen, about how cute I thought Jessica was (even though that might not have been so relevant), and about the bottle of FV, which I carefully produced from my backpack. Then, when I was all through, Gramps one-upped me.

"The PWO." Gramps shook his head. "I didn't know they still existed."

"You know about the PWO?" I was shocked.

"I know all about those conniving principals," Gramps signed.

I was on the edge of my seat.

"The Principals' World Order," Gramps leaned back in his chair as he signed, "was formed hundreds and hundreds, maybe even thousands, of years ago by the loyal followers of Baron Edgar von Principales, who preached that civilization would crumble because of children and their desire to have fun.

" 'Kids don't work,' von Principales noted. 'They don't vote. They don't provide for themselves or for others. They have no responsibilities. They don't just crave fun, they feel entitled to it.'

"According to von Principales, kids believe that life is, and should always be, fun. When there's no fun to be had, they stomp their feet, they scream, they rant, they rave, and they cry until some poor adult with a splitting headache is forced to entertain them. So the baron concluded that the spirit of childhood needed to be broken. Fun had to be removed from the world.

" 'But how?' his students asked. To answer, the baron asked his disciples to imagine a place where responsible adults could systematically break the spirit of childhood day in and day out; a place where childish games and antics would be replaced by boring lessons; a place where rigid regulations would rule and where children would be harshly punished for breaking rank; in short, a place that would eliminate fun from the world. Baron von Principales felt that these institutions should be opened in every town in the world.

"Many thought the baron was crazy, but before he died, his vision was realized. Days before he was eaten by a family of hungry bears, the first 'School,' which literally translated means 'Box of Torture' in Baron von Principales' native language, opened its doors to an army of kids who would have rather been somewhere else having fun.

"Though he died early, his concept spread over the globe like wildfire. Before anyone knew it, there was a school in every town, just as the baron had envisioned. And each school was run by a single man or woman who was loyal to the baron's greatest belief: Kids Stink!"

"That's why they're called principals," I said. "They followed von Principales!"

"Exactly," Gramps signed. "The PWO formed to ensure that every principal would act to stifle fun. After the death of von Principales, the principals selected a principal principal to assume the baron's role, and his motto became known as the Principal Principals' Principle. Since that time, who knows how many principal principals have worn the Ring of the Chained Child?"

"Are all principals in the PWO?" I asked.

"Not anymore," Gramps explained. "The world lost track of the original purpose of von Principales' schools, just as we have lost track of the original purpose of so many things. In fact, much to the horror of the original principals, kids quickly turned schools into institutions of fun. Even more insulting to the legacy of the baron, these very kids grew up to become principals.

"Outnumbered by kindhearted, fun-loving principals, the followers of von Principales went underground, reaffirmed their allegiance to squelching kids' fun, and conceived Formula FV, a vaccine for fun. Comparatively few in number, the PWO's greatest strength came from their secrecy. You could never tell just by looking at a principal if he or she was one of the good ones or one of the evil ones.

"It has been so long since I've heard of any PWO activity that I just assumed the last of its members had died off. But from what you have witnessed this week, Meatball, clearly, the PWO is alive and well."

"How do you know all this?" I wondered.

"When I was a child, back in the small town of Uksnookalackerliski, where I grew up, in Russia, I heard many stories about the PWO, but I believed they were just that—stories that parents scared their kids with. So, on my tenth birthday, I brought my classmates birthday blintzes to eat and Pin the Tail on the Potato to play during recess. When my principal saw us laughing and celebrating, he dragged me by my hair into his office. Unfortunately for me, not only was my principal a card-carrying member of the PWO, he was being visited and reviewed that day by the principal principal himself.

"Under the watchful eyes of the principal principal, my principal had to demonstrate his allegiance to the PPP more than ever.

" 'Mister Finkelstein,' he barked at me to his principal principal's delight, "for attempting to bring fun into the hallways and classrooms of my school, you must be punished. Stand up and face the wall!' I did as I was told, and my principal picked up two wooden paddles and smashed them into my ears. Of course, this would never be tolerated today. But it was eighty-seven years ago, and

I was forced to suffer several blows to each ear. The last sound I heard in my life was the giddy laughter of the reigning principal principal."

32

I entered my apartment to the sound of Precious screaming at my mom and dad about how they'd ruined her perfect life. Apparently, while I'd been busy creating a formula to rid children from the world and uncovering the diabolical plot to use it, Precious's furniture had been taken away. I had a sudden urge to test out the FV on my sister. It would serve her right, I figured. But I decided it would be a waste since there was absolutely nothing fun about her to begin with.

Safe inside my bedless bedroom, I carefully removed the FV from my backpack, placed it on the floor in front of me, and wondered what to do. The soda bottle I now possessed contained enough formula to wipe every child off the face of the planet. Clearly, this wasn't something I could just toss in the garbage.

From behind the FV, on the floor where my desk had once stood, a blinking light on my computer screen caught my eye. An e-mail waited for me. I crawled over to my computer and discovered that it wasn't just any old piece of mail, it was a message from theWeaselman@PWO.com.

Dear Mizterrr Finkelztein,

Surely you don't think I had you make all that Formula FV juzt to help improve yourrr gradez. That vould be rrridiculouz, yez no? The FV waz suppozed to be forrr me and my friendz, and ve vant it back. Now!

Howeverrr, ve at the PWO are not unreazonable. Ve don't expect to get something forrr nothing. So, here'z what ve propoze: If you bring back the FV that ve know you have, ve vill rrreturn yourrr friendz Max Lichtenztein and Jezzica George to yourrr cuztody. It'z a good deal, Mizterrr Finkelztein. Ve're offerring two forrr the price of one.

Howeverrr, to sveeten the pot, ve also have yourrr old friend Rrrufuz Delaney, who waz kind enough to tell his mom what he saw flying out of my vindow. If you get the FV to uz before eight o'clock, Mrs. Delaney haz offered to tezt it on young Rrrufuz forrr no extra charge. That'z a great value. But act now, az thiz offerrr vill not lazt!

After infecting my computer with a virus that promptly ate the contents of my hard drive, the Weasel-man's message deleted itself.

I obviously had to save Max and Jessica, but I couldn't just give the FV back to the PWO. I needed a plan. Actually, the plan came to me pretty quickly. What I really needed was someone to help me execute it.

Normally, that someone would be Max, but clearly, that was out of the question. Gramps was way too old to get involved in all this. Mom and Dad were far too likely to kill me. There was only one place for me to turn.

I stepped out into the hallway. It was quiet. The fight between Precious and Mom and Dad was apparently over and there was no sign of anyone. Mom and Dad had ducked out for a moment. I pushed open my sister's door.

"Precious," I said to her back, "I need help."

She stayed put, her back to me. I took several brave steps into her room, stepping over the piles of clothes and books and stuff that covered her furnitureless floor.

"You're the only person I can turn to," I explained.

She turned around and swung at me with her field hockey stick.

I dodged the attack. "Will you stop it?" I yelled. "I need your help!"

She dropped the field hockey stick.

"Thank you," I sighed.

She picked up her lacrosse stick, which was several inches longer.

"Don't you want to help your baby brother out?" I appealed to her softer side, not that I had ever seen evidence that she had one.

She charged at me like a bull with a sword. I barely managed to step out of the way.

"Come on," I pleaded. "Don't you care about me deep, deep, deep, deep, deep, deep, deep, deep down inside?"

She scooped an apple off the floor with her lacrosse stick and aimed it at my head. It smashed into the wall behind me, splattering juice all over the back of my neck.

"Believe me," I panted, "I wouldn't be here if I didn't have to be. This wasn't Plan A, sis. This wasn't even Plan B or C. This is like Plan Z. I'm desperate."

She tilted her head to the side a bit and looked at me. I was finally getting through.

"What do you say?" I begged. "Will you help me?"

She shrugged, took a nice deep breath, and whipped the lacrosse stick at me. It smacked into my head and knocked me to the floor.

"Meatball!" Precious screamed. "Are you okay?"

I wasn't, but I smiled anyway. "You spoke to me. I knew you liked me."

"Darn it!" Precious screamed, and she kicked me in the shin.

"Help me," I pleaded, rubbing my head with one hand and my shin with the other.

She just stood there.

"What if I do something for you in exchange?"

"What could *you* possibly do for *me*?" she sneered.

Without even knowing I knew it, I knew what I could do. "If you help me," I groaned as I tried to stand up, "I'll get all our stuff back and fix it so we won't have to move, we won't have to share a room, and nothing else will get in the way of your perfectly precious life."

"You're going to do all that?" Precious tittered. "How?"

I told her what I had in mind.

"You know," she acknowledged, "for a real bonehead, that's not such a boneheaded idea. So what do I have to do?"

After a quick rundown on what had happened so far and who we were about to butt heads with, she agreed to help me, largely because she didn't believe a word I said.

As we headed out, my parents were heading back in with a woman in thick black-rimmed glasses who was carrying a briefcase.

"Where are you two off to?" my mom asked, instinctively on to us.

"Gramps's."

"Who's she?" Precious asked.

"Joanna St. Onge." The woman grabbed Precious's hand and nearly shook it off her arm. "Number one real estate agent in Manhattan. Well, uptown. Well, Upper East Side. Well, number one real estate agent between Seventy-first and Seventy-fourth streets."

Precious pulled her hand back from Ms. St. Onge's.

My dad laughed. My mom shot him a look; then she shot Precious a look; then she led the agent into our apartment.

We really did stop at Gramps's place first. We had an important assignment for him.

"When Mom and Dad come down here to get us, cover for us. And when Mom doesn't believe you, keep lying."

"Sure thing," Gramps signed. He later told me that of all the insane things that happened that week, seeing me and Precious joined together on a mission, of our own free will, took the cake.

"We'll see you after we save Max and Jessica."

"Try not to eliminate fun from the planet while you're at it."

Precious and I headed downstairs and flagged a cab to take us to school.

"Hey," I asked Precious, "you know I've been eating meat, don't you?"

"Of course."

"Well, why haven't you told Mom and Dad?"

"I haven't told Mom and Dad *yet*," Precious explained. "I've been waiting for the moment when it would do the most damage to you."

"That makes sense," I thought. The cab pulled up in front of the school.

My plan was to be in and out of the PWO headquarters in less than three minutes, with Precious, Max, Jessica, and the FV. As for Rufus Delaney, I'd have to see how I was feeling at the time. Maybe I'd take him with me too, but I doubted it.

34

"Why are we in a filthy out-of-order bathroom?" Precious asked. "If this is some kind of joke, I'll kill you. Literally."

I didn't answer, I just turned the cold water faucet on. The bathroom plummeted beneath the school. Precious looked shocked. She was finally beginning to believe me. A moment later, the elevator came to a stop, and we stepped out into the wet, chalk dust–smelling hallway and made our way around its curves, twists, bends, and turns without uttering a word.

At the last bend before the PWO headquarters, I pulled Precious back into the shadows. Up ahead, several principals, dressed in the dark gray suits and the dark gray ties of the PWO, waited by the massive open doors. The principals all referred to each other by the numbers stitched onto their lapels.

"How long until he gets here, Principal 7?" the woman with the number 473 on her collar asked.

"Any time now, Principal 473," Principal 7 responded.

"That is," Principal 64 laughed, "if he has the guts to show."

"The principal principal said the boy's coming," Principal 298 barked, "so he's coming."

Precious grabbed my hand. "You weren't lying." She was quivering. "There *is* a PWO, its headquarters *are* under our school, and you *actually* want me to go in there with you."

"Yep." I clenched her hand tight. "You're going to be great, Precious, perfect."

"What exactly is Plan Z?"

I pulled out a meatball and handed the backpack to my sister. "Put this on," I said. "And don't take it off until I tell you to, okay?"

"Okay." Precious nodded. Being scared out of her mind suited my sister well.

"Are you ready?"

Precious said "Yes" but shook her head "No."

I popped the meatball into my mouth, changed shape, grabbed my sister by her wrist, looked down at her, and squealed, "Ve only have two minutez and thirty-nine secondz. Let'z go."

Though clearly confused, the principals on guard stood at attention and saluted when they saw me approaching.

"We didn't see you leave, Principal Principal," Principal 473 commented.

"I vent out to nab anotherrr one of theze vile creaturez to sveeten the pot forrr ourrr friend Mizterrr Finkelztein."

The principals on guard laughed.

"You are truly a maniacal genius, Principal Principal," Principal 7 said, kissing up to me.

"When you'rrre good, you'rrre good." I winked, then clicked my heels and proceeded into the PWO headquarters, Precious at my side.

The room we entered was large, concrete, and filled with the type of computer consoles you'd expect to find in a place like NASA. The technicians at the computers were busily preparing to remove fun from the world. Precious and I ducked down behind an unmanned console before we were spotted. A few seconds later, I became me again. We crawled along to the end of the console. The principal principal's voice rang out of the next room, but our view was blocked by a ten-foot pile of boxes labeled PROPERTY OF THE PTA.

"We have to get over there." I pointed across the fifteen or so exposed feet between us and the boxes.

"Why?" Precious demanded. "I'm perfectly happy right here."

"But we can't see anything from here."

"So?" Precious really didn't want to leave our hiding spot.

"We're going over there."

"No we're not." Precious shook her head.

"Give me your hand or I'll have to leave you here by yourself."

That convinced her. We made a break for it, and before Precious knew it, we were safely hidden behind the stack of PTA boxes.

From our new position, we could see right into the room where the Weasel-man anxiously awaited my arrival. The word STRATEGY was written above the open door. The walls of the room were covered with maps of the world. Pins stuck in the map marked the location of every school on the planet.  The secondary principal, a man they called the tertiary principal, and Mrs. Delaney paced in the footsteps of their principal principal, waiting for me to deliver the FV. Max, Jessica, and Rufus sat in the middle of the room, chained to writing desks seemingly salvaged from a medieval torture chamber's going-out-of-business sale.

"All right," I assured my sister, "all we have to do is stick to the plan and we'll be out of here before you know it. Give me the backpack."

35

Precious walked straight into the strategy room with the Fun Vaccine in her hands.

"And what do ve have herrre?" the principal principal squealed.

"Hello, Principal Weaselman." My sister smiled. "Meatball came down with a cold, so my parents won't let him leave the house. He asked me to give you this stuff and pick up his friends for him."

The tertiary principal took the bottle and handed it to the secondary principal, who handed it to the principal principal, who examined the merchandise and squealed, "Very good. This is what I vanted."

"Um . . ." Precious glanced at her watch. "Can I have them now?"

"Prezident Delaney, rrreleaze thoze annoying little varmintz. I vouldn't vant them to mizz out on the lazt dayz of childhood."

Mrs. Delaney unchained Jessica, Max, and Rufus. "Come on, guys." Precious was looking at her watch again. "We should go. Now!" Rufus just stood there by his mother's side, while Max and Jessica, sensing that something was in the works, did as they were told. They just didn't do it fast enough.

They weren't even close to the door when the bottle of FV that Principal Weaselman was cradling like a baby turned back into me.

"Stop thoze kidz!" he shouted, and tightened his grip around my wrist. The secondary and tertiary principals grabbed Max and Jessica. Reinforcements appeared and nabbed my sister. Mrs. Delaney grabbed her son.

"Mom," Rufus pleaded, "please tell me what's going on here."

"Be quiet," Mrs. Delaney ordered. "And stop calling me Mom."

As any decent strategist will tell you, all good plans involve equally good backup plans. Though I was an amateur, I am happy to say that I had a pretty good backup plan. I had a meatball in my pocket, which I was already cradling with my free hand.

"Where'z my FV?" the Weasel-man thundered.

"Well," I said, stalling, "that's an interesting story, you see—"

"You," the principal said to Principal 416, "take the girl Jezzica and rrrip out her hairrr!"

"Yes, Principal Principal," Principal 416 dutifully replied. With no time to spare, I pulled the meatball out of my pocket. Somewhere between my pocket and my mouth, though, Mrs. Delaney intercepted it. She took great delight in dropping it into the garbage can.

"Principal 416," the principal principal barked, "herrr hairrr!"

As any decent strategist will tell you, all good backup plans involve equally good backup-backup plans. And, though I was an amateur, I am happy to say that I had a pretty good backup-backup plan. There was another meatball in my sister's pocket. With everyone focused on Principal 416 as he closed in on Jessica, Precious seized the opportunity to sink her teeth into the arm of one of her captors, forcing him to let go long enough for her to grab the meatball in her pocket and throw it to me.

Suddenly all eyes, including Principal 416's, were on the flying meatball. The throw was perfect. After all, this is Precious we're talking about. My mouth was wide open, poised to catch the meatball. At the last minute, though, Principal Weaselman's mouth somehow ended up in front of mine. He swallowed my meatball without even taking a bite.

As any decent strategist will tell you, all good backup-backup plans involve equally good backup-backup-backup plans. Unfortunately, I was only an amateur, and I am sad to say that I had no backup-backup-backup plan. We were doomed.

"Principal 416," the Weasel-man raged, "pull out herrr hairrr!"

"Wait!" I yelled, caving. "I'll give you the FV."

"Principal 416." The principal principal held up a finger. "One moment, pleaze."

Jessica let out a deep sigh of relief.

"Where iz it?"

"In the other room," I admitted.

"You vill take me there now!" The principal principal pushed me into the outer room.

I squeezed behind the stack of PTA boxes and grabbed my backpack. Principal Weaselman immediately snatched it from me and shoved me back into the strategy room. He searched the bag for hidden meatballs. When he realized that there weren't any, he pulled out the soda bottle. Unfortunately for me, Precious, Jessica, Max, Rufus, and every other kid on the planet, that bottle actually was filled with the real Fun Vaccine.

36

"Well," I suggested, "You got your FV, Principal Weaselman, so I guess we'll just get out of the way and—"

The principal principal stepped in front of the door. "Afterrr the stunt you juzt tried to pull, you can't expect me to believe that this is rrreally the FV."

"But it is!" I exclaimed. "Really!"

"Mizterrr Finkelztein, surrrely I do not need to tell you of all people that lookz can be deceiving, yez no?"

"Yes, they can," I admitted, "but in this case they're not. That's the real FV."

"Ve shall see about that. You, Prinzipal 319, bring me Mizterrr Delaney."

The man with 319 stitched onto his lapel dragged Rufus over to the Weasel-man.

"Mom," Rufus whimpered, "help me."

"Rufus," Mrs. Delaney said, smiling, "this is going to hurt me more than it's going to hurt you."

"Really?" Rufus moaned.

After a moment of consideration, his mom admitted, "No."

"Why are you doing this?" Rufus yelled.

"For the same reason I adopted you. To serve my principal principal."

"I'm adopted?" Rufus sniffled.

"Ten years ago," Mrs. Delaney explained, "Principal Principal Weaselman came to me to say that I, and a few of my colleagues, would better serve the PWO if we infiltrated the PTA. That day, I went straight to an adoption agency and took the first kid they offered. You."

"Enough blabbering!" the principal principal hollered, and he ordered Principal 319 to "Hold him still!"

Principal 319 clasped onto Rufus's shoulders and held him in front of the principal principal.

"Droperrr!" demanded the principal principal.

"Dropper!" shouted the secondary principal.

"Dropper!" announced the tertiary principal, and he handed the secondary principal an eyedropper.

"Dropper!" proclaimed the secondary principal as he passed it along to his leader.

The principal principal carefully twisted the cap off the soda bottle and delicately removed a single drop of the green, phlegmy FV. He screwed the cap back on and put the bottle aside.

"Vell, Mizterrr Delaney, you lucky boy. The horrible fun of childhood vill soon be a diztant memory." The principal principal held the eyedropper above Rufus's head. We all watched as the green droplet fell off the tip of the eyedropper, plummeted through the air, and splashed into Rufus Delaney's hair.

The principal principal took a step away from Rufus. Principal 319 did the same. The rest of us just stood there, waiting for something to happen.

"Ohhhh," Rufus groaned, "I don't feel so good."

A growth spurt shook his right leg, which sprouted inches in less than a second. His now stumpy left leg dangled in the air. There was a popping noise, and the left leg instantly caught up with the right one. Rufus's arms stretched out. His torso grew. A gut bulged out from underneath his shirt, while up on his head his hair receded. A wrinkle appeared across his forehead, followed by several more around his eyes. A tacky mustache sprouted above his lips, and a blue-and-gray-striped bow tie tied itself around his neck. His sneakers turned into loafers, a briefcase appeared in one of his hairy hands, and thick glasses formed on his aged face.

"Ha!" cried the principal principal. "It vorkz! The Fun Vaczine vorkz!" He turned to Rufus, smiled, and said, "Excuze me, sir. Vould you mind telling me, what iz yourrr name?"

"Forgive me," the adult Rufus responded in a

scratchy, deep voice, "where are my manners today?" He pulled a business card out of his pocket, handed it to the principal principal, and introduced himself. "I'm Rufus H. Delaney, attorney-at-law. Pleasure to make your acquaintance."

"Bring me Miz Finkelztein!" the principal principal ordered.

"Hold on," I pleaded. "The FV works. You have to let us go. That was the deal!"

"Waz it? The girrrl," he shrieked.

"What exactly is going on here?" Rufus H. Delaney butted in, his keen legal mind detecting that something was amiss.

"Nothing that concernz you, Mizterrr Delaney. Principal 204, pleaze see our friend out." Principal 204 marched the forty-year-old balding Rufus out and slammed the door.

The principal principal refilled the eyedropper and grabbed hold of my sister.

"No!" I yelled. I attempted to break free from

the principals who were holding me, but I couldn't shake them off. Jessica couldn't escape from her captors' grasps either. But for some reason, there was only one principal holding Max. I can only guess that the logic was—why would you possibly need two men to hold one one-armed kid? Because, as Max demonstrated for everyone, a one-armed kid could easily lift one of his two knees straight up and into his captor's unmentionables. The principal holding Max fell to the floor, crippled with pain.

As the Weasel-man squeezed out a drop of the Fun Vaccine over Precious's head, Max barreled across the room. The moment before the vaccine landed on my sister's head, Max knocked her out of the way. The only problem was, the drop of FV was now heading for Max, who stood in Precious's place. It would have hit him, too, if not for that darn missing arm. The FV fell right on that spot where the rest of us have right arms but where Max has nothing. It continued straight toward the ground. But something else got in its way.

"Thiz iz an unfortunate turn of eventz," Principal Weaselman whimpered when the drop of Fun Vaccine landed on his foot.

All the principals in the room ran to their leader's side. Precious grabbed Max and pulled him over to Jessica and me.

"Let's get out of here!" Jessica whispered.

"How?" Precious asked. "There are more principals out there." She pointed out the door. "We'll never make it."

"Someone grab the FV," I instructed. "I'll get us a ride."

While the frenzied principals waited to see what effect the vaccine would have on their leader, Precious snagged the bottle of FV. I had the grimmer task of fishing the meatball Mrs. Delaney had discarded out of the trash and eating it. It certainly didn't taste good, but it did the trick. Jessica, Max, Precious, and the Fun Vaccine all rode right out of the PWO headquarters in a state-of-the-art tank that previously had existed only in my own Rufus Delaney revenge fantasies.

"Tonight's top story"—every news anchor in town reported the same thing that night—"takes us deep inside the minds of three master criminals. Earlier today, every news organization in the city received this videotape from an anonymous source."

A man who looked like a bowling ball appeared on the television.

"My name iz Valrrruz Doubleju Veazelman, though my colleaguez know me az the prinzipal prinzipal. I am the maztermind behind a diabolical plan to rrrid the planet of children. Howeverrr, I can no longerrr live with myzelf and with my evil vays. I am overcome vith shame."

The Weasel-man's unsolicited confession went on to provide key details about the FV, the PWO, the PPP, and the PTA.

"In clozing"—the Weasel-man shed a tear—"I vould like to rrrezign my pozition az prinzipal of Parkman Juniorrr High. Thank you." He abruptly stepped off camera.

"I have been a blind follower of the PWO, the PPP, and the principal principal for all my adult life," the secondary principal began. "And I am not alone. I am just one of the 679 principals of the PWO. But don't take my word for it. Go see for yourself. Our headquarters are underneath Parkman Junior High." After giving thorough directions on how to find the PWO headquarters, the secondary principal quickly stepped off camera too.

"My name is Mrs. Delaney, and I have been the president of the Parkman PTA for seven years now. However, I, too, am loyal to the PWO. Years ago, several of my colleagues and I infiltrated PTAs the world over. As the PTA president of the school run by the principal principal himself, it has been my responsibility to coordinate with the other planted PTA presidents and keep them up to date on PWO orders." After a heartfelt resignation and apology from Mrs. Delaney, the tape abruptly stopped. In an odd coincidence, it was later discovered that each of the three confessions had occurred in just under two minutes and thirty-nine seconds.

"In a related story," anchormen and -women reported that night, "the secondary principal and Mrs. Delaney were apprehended earlier this evening by local authorities. Hoping to take the PWO by surprise, a New York City SWAT team was forced to dig through the floor of an uptown grocery store to reach a sewage pipe connecting to their target. In their haste, however, the SWAT team accidentally took out one of the market's key structural support walls." A live shot of a burning pile of concrete and debris that had once been Super Health splashed across the screen. "Several principals were taken in the raid, though many fled the scene and are still at large at this hour. Presumably, the principal principal is among those who escaped, as no one has located him yet."

In a seemingly unrelated story later in the newscast that I happened to be watching that night, one commentator reported that New York City's Child Services had found a confused boy wandering the streets.

"The twelve-year-old boy was found with no possessions aside from a silver ring engraved with the bizarre image of a crying child in chains. The boy, Wally W. Weaselman, claimed that he is actually a fifty-six-year-old man. After hours of intense psychological research conducted earlier this evening, young Wally Weaselman has been remanded to the Sunshine Orphanage for Wayward Boys, *a place where kids can just be kids and have some fun!* We wish you the best of luck, Wally."

Notably, the Fun Vaccine that the principal principal referred to during his confession was never recovered. Most people doubt that it ever existed. But it did. In fact, it still does, though there are only two people on this planet who know where it is.

Jess and I invited Max and Precious to the secret ceremonial burial of the soda bottle, but they were on their way to a movie together. It's been four

days and counting since Precious stopped the Meatball Acknowledgment Embargo, and I doubt she'll ever start it again. I don't think she could go a day without telling me, once more, about how the most perfect thing she ever saw in her entire life was the way that drop of FV narrowly missed Max as he saved her life. There's no question in Precious's mind. Max is perfect. I wouldn't be surprised if she married him one day. After all, you know how my sister feels about perfection.

That about wraps it up, which means that I can finally make good on that promise I made to Precious. I told her if she helped me out, I'd find a way to get our things back and save us and the house from Mom and Dad's *adult problems*. Thanks to you, Ms. Capriotti, and the rest of you big-time Delacorte Press book editors, not only did I do that, I saved myself from certain death. Right before I confessed to my parents that I had been eating meat all week, I handed them the $37,816.14 you sent me as payment for the rights to my story. Though my mother did try to convince me that if we were supposed to eat meat, animals would be stuffed with bread crumbs instead of organs, I ended up convincing her and my dad that if I wasn't supposed to eat meat, broccoli would give me super-powers. As soon as the check clears, you can feel free to publish this.

In the meantime, I have a date with Jessica I should get ready for. I offered to turn myself into a limousine to pick her up, but she wasn't interested, because of all the things I can become, she says she likes me best as a Meatball.

What a girl!

Sincerely,

Meatball Finkelstein

Meatball Finkelstein

P.S. If you have any further questions, please feel free to contact my lawyer, Rufus H. Delaney.

About the Author

One day, Ross Venokur was sitting in a coffee shop working on a book when a remarkably round boy approached him and asked, "Are you Ross Venokur, author of *The Amazing Frecktackle* and *The Cookie Company*?"

"Why, yes," Ross modestly replied. "I am."

That round boy turned out to be Meatball Finkelstein. After hearing his incredible story, Ross was so honored that Meatball had asked for his assistance in writing his autobiography that he threw away his nearly finished novel to get started immediately.

"Working with Meatball has been the greatest joy of my life," Ross recently remarked to a group of tourists he mistook for news reporters.

Ross and his wife, Lenore, are currently being evicted from their home in Santa Monica, California, because they refuse to get rid of their dog, Sampson. They hope to have a new residence before Ross's next book comes out.